A Robyn Hunter Mystery

Shadow of Doubt

NORAH McCLINTOCK

Scholastic Canada Ltd.
Toronto New York London Auckland Sydney
Mexico City New Delhi Hong Kong Buenos Aires

Scholastic Canada Ltd.
604 King Street West, Toronto, Ontario M5V 1E1, Canada

Scholastic Inc.
557 Broadway, New York, NY 10012, USA

Scholastic Australia Pty Limited
PO Box 579, Gosford, NSW 2250, Australia

Scholastic New Zealand Limited
Private Bag 94407, Greenmount, Auckland, New Zealand

Scholastic Children's Books
Euston House, 24 Eversholt Street, London NW1 1DB, UK

Library and Archives Canada Cataloguing in Publication
McClintock, Norah
Shadow of doubt / Norah McClintock.
(A Robyn Hunter mystery)
ISBN 978-0-545-99729-4

I. Title. II. Series: McClintock, Norah. Robyn Hunter mystery
PS8575.C62S53 2008   jC813'.54   C2007-907197-X
ISBN-10 0-545-99729-1

Cover photo by Catherine London.

6 5 4 3 2 1   Printed in Canada   08 09 10 11 12

To complex kids everywhere

Chapter 1

The man sitting across the table from me was named Charlie Hart. I had met him many times before. He used to work with my father. They were still friends. Sometimes Charlie Hart and my father had dinner together. Sometimes Charlie Hart showed up at one of my father's parties — my father loves to throw parties. Sometimes my father and Charlie Hart played poker together. But today Charlie Hart was working.

My parents were somewhere outside, waiting for me. At first my mother wanted to come in with me. But I told her no, it was okay, I could answer all of the questions without her because, after all, I was the one who had been there, not her. She had finally agreed, but I could tell she was upset because she didn't automatically get up and move one place over when my father sat down next to her. They're divorced.

The table between Charlie Hart and me was bare except for a can of ginger ale in front of me and a cup of coffee in front of him. He took a sip of his coffee and asked me how my father was. When I told him that my father had just come back from a couple of weeks in Europe, Charlie Hart said, "Some guys have all the luck." He asked me how school was going. I said it was okay. He asked me about the "young fellow" who had been with me the last time he had seen me. "Is he your boyfriend?" he said. I shrugged but didn't answer. Some things are personal. Charlie Hart didn't push me on it. He said, "I'm going to videotape this, Robyn. Okay?"

I said okay.

He said the date and the time and who was in the room — which was just the two of us — and then he said, "I want you to tell me everything you can about what happened today and everything you can remember about the events leading up to today."

"Everything?" I said. That covered a lot of territory.

"Everything," Charlie Hart said. He sat forward in his chair and watched me with sharp eyes that reminded me of my father's. My father used to be a cop. Charlie Hart still was a cop.

Chapter 2

Ms Denholm was young, attractive, creative, enthusiastic, and funny — in other words, she was the kind of person who, when you met her, you immediately asked yourself, What is she doing here?, *here* being a high-school classroom. Ms Denholm was an English teacher. She was substituting for Ms March, my regular English teacher, who had gone on maternity leave before Christmas. Ms Denholm was standing in front of the chalkboard, announcing that she would be directing the annual school play.

"Sign up for auditions if you're interested," she said. "And by the way, people, there's as much drama backstage as there is onstage, so if you don't see yourself as the next Scarlett Johansson or Brad Pitt, why not find out how much they rely on the behind-the-scenes professionals who are responsible for sets, costumes, lighting, props . . . well, you get the picture." Here Ms Denholm flashed a mega-watt smile, complete with charming dimples, that made my best

3

friend Billy Royal turn to mush and my other best friend Morgan Turner, Billy's girlfriend, turn to stone.

"Who does she think she's kidding?" Morgan said between classes, after Billy had printed his name neatly under the heading *Sets*. "Anyone can slap paint on plywood. Not anyone can be a movie star." She looked daggers at Billy, who grinned back, not understanding that she was taking a dig at him because, really, it would never occur to Billy to want to be a movie star. I doubt movie stars even registered on his radar. Billy isn't much of a people person. He's more of an animal person. A Jacques Cousteau kind of guy. Someone who is far more likely to admire William Lishman, the man who taught some orphaned geese to migrate, than he is to admire Brad Pitt.

"So you're not going to sign up?" I said to Morgan. I had taken the pen from Billy and put my name down under *Props and Set Dressing*.

Morgan snatched the pen from my hand and inscribed her name in big, bold block letters right under Billy's. She would never in a million years have admitted it to him, but she was crazy about Billy, so crazy that she was actually jealous of Ms Denholm — a teacher.

* * *

During my fourth-period spare that afternoon, I happened to be walking past the school office when Ms Nettleworth, one of the school's administrative assistants, rapped on the floor-to-ceiling glass that separates the office from the hall. She beckoned me inside.

"Do me a favour, Robyn," she said, peering at me

over the top of the reading glasses that hung from a chain over her large bosom when they weren't perched on the tip of her sharp nose. "Take this box up to Ms Denholm."

The box was long and narrow and white and was fastened with a red ribbon that had been fashioned into a huge bow.

"Flowers," I said.

"So it would appear," Ms Nettleworth said, tapping the label that was affixed to one corner of the box. The words *Garden of Eden* were printed on it, next to a little drawing of a bouquet of flowers. "They were on the counter when I came back from lunch, but I haven't had time to deliver them. Ruth's out with the flu, and I'm swamped." Ruth Grier was the school's other administrative assistant. "Ms Denholm has a spare period now. If she isn't in her classroom, she'll be in the teachers' lounge."

In fact, Ms Denholm was sitting at her desk at the front of her classroom. She waved me in when I knocked. Her eyes went straight to the box in my hands. I hadn't had any personal experience with the type of box I was carrying, but I had seen my mother eye boxes just like it. She always looked pleasantly surprised, even delighted, to see such a box being carried in her direction (unless, of course, she suspected that it had been sent by my father). She always smiled. Women, my mother says, love to receive flowers (unless, she invariably adds, they're from an ex-husband who is having trouble accepting that he is, in fact, ex).

But Ms Denholm did not smile. If anything, she looked suspicious.

"What's that?" she said.

"Flowers, I think," I said. "Ms Nettleworth asked me to bring them up to you." I walked toward her. She jumped up out of her chair when I set the box in front of her, as if she were convinced that it was full of snakes.

"Who would send me flowers?" she said.

She was asking *me?*

"Is it your birthday?" I said.

She shook her head. "And I haven't lived here very long. I barely know anyone." She peered at the box but didn't touch it.

"There's a card." I pointed to a small envelope tucked under the ribbon. Ms Denholm's name was printed on the front of it.

She plucked the envelope out from under the ribbon. Her hands shook as she opened it. She frowned. The envelope was empty.

"Open the box," she said.

"But they're for you."

"Please," she said, without looking at me. Her eyes were on the box.

I slipped off the ribbon, lifted the lid, and began to part the tissue paper inside. It was black — an odd choice of colour, I thought.

"Oh," I said, stunned by what I saw. I looked at Ms Denholm.

Her face had turned the colour of milk. She grasped the back of her chair to steady herself.

"Is there a note in there?" she said.

I looked into the box again. It contained a dozen red roses — they were gorgeous. Nestled among them was a baby doll. Its chest had been ripped open and it was splattered with what looked like blood but was probably red paint. Its head was missing. I lifted it out of the box and gingerly poked among the thorns.

"No note," I said.

Ms Denholm snatched the lid off the desk where I had set it, jammed it back on, and threw the box into the wastepaper basket that sat on the floor beside her desk.

"Maybe you should call the police," I said.

"The police?" The disdain in her voice made it clear what she thought of that idea. "Do you know what they'd say? That someone is playing a practical joke on me and that practical jokes aren't against the law. Or they'd ask me if any of my students has something against me — did I criticize someone in front of the class? Did I grade someone too hard?" Bitterness robbed her voice of the musical quality it normally had. She drew in a deep breath and slowly straightened up. She tried to smile, but her face looked strained. "That's probably all it is," she said. "Someone's idea of a joke. A bad joke, if you ask me. But it's probably harmless." She didn't look convinced — or sound convincing. "Let's just forget it happened, okay, Robyn?"

Reluctantly, I agreed. But I had the feeling that this wasn't the first time that something like this had happened to Ms Denholm.

* * *

There are two kinds of kids who take art class at my school: those who think that art is an easy credit and those who are genuinely talented. Both groups make the art room one of the most interesting classrooms in the school. There are always new creations on the walls and new works-in-progress scattered throughout the room. Some of them are howlingly awful, and therefore worth checking out. Others are astonishingly accomplished, and therefore also worth a look. When I pass the art room, which I do regularly on my way to my locker, I usually glance inside.

That afternoon when I looked in, Ms Denholm was there with Ms Rachlis, the substitute art teacher who was filling in while Ms Pinelli, the regular art teacher, recovered from an accident — apparently she'd had a nasty fall down three flights of concrete stairs in her apartment building. Ms Denholm and Ms Rachlis were both looking at a box that was sitting in the middle of Ms Rachlis's desk. It was the same long white flower box that I had delivered to Ms Denholm earlier that afternoon. Ms Rachlis reached in and pulled out the headless doll. She examined it and said something to Ms Denholm. Then she opened her desk drawer and pulled out some tissues. She handed them to Ms Denholm, who wiped her eyes and shook her head. She had told me that she was sure the flowers were a harmless joke, but she obviously didn't believe it. I hoped Ms Rachlis would convince her to do what I had already suggested: call the police.

Ms Rachlis turned toward the door. I scurried away. I don't think either of them saw me.

* * *

"It doesn't surprise me," Morgan said when I told her about the flowers and the headless doll over latte (for her) and hot chocolate (for me) at our favourite coffee shop after school. "It's probably a drop-dead offering from some woman whose boyfriend she stole." She was still annoyed at the way Billy had looked at Ms Denholm.

"Morgan, you should have seen how upset she was. She was in tears. *And* she looked scared," I said.

"But she didn't want to call the cops?"

I shook my head. "That seemed like the last thing she wanted to do."

"See?" Morgan said. "What did I tell you? People always have a reason when they don't want to get the cops involved. I bet you anything that I'm right. I bet she used those dimples of hers to steal some other woman's boyfriend." Her eyes skipped from me to someplace over my shoulder. "Speaking of boy-friends," she said, grinning at someone behind me, "here comes one."

"Billy?"

"Not my boyfriend, Robyn. Yours."

My heart raced. My whole body tingled. I knew, of course, that I was being stupid, that I was setting myself up for disappointment. But in the split second before I whirled around, I imagined that the person behind me would be Nick.

It wasn't.

It was Ben.

Sweet Ben Logan, according to Morgan. Considerate Ben Logan. Movie-star-handsome Ben Logan.

And, according to Morgan, my boyfriend.

I shoved aside my disappointment, plastered a smile onto my face, and said, "Hi" in the perkiest tone I could muster. It shouldn't have been difficult. After all, Ben really was sweet. He really was considerate. And he really was cute. When he slipped an arm around me, pulled me close, and bent to kiss my cheek, the rush of excitement that surged through me almost made me forget Nick. Almost, but not quite. Not yet. I told myself it was just a matter of time before I got over Nick. I told myself that I couldn't spend the rest of my life waiting for him to pop back into my life again after suddenly popping out of it without any warning. I told myself that I was lucky to have Ben, who would never in a million years do what Nick had done.

"What are you doing here, Ben?" I said. "How did you know where to find me?"

"Hmmm," he said, frowning slightly. "It's after school, you're best friends with a caffeine addict — "

"Hey," Morgan protested. "*Addict* is such a values-laden word."

"And," Ben said, "this is the closest place to your school to get a decent latte."

"You've got that right," Morgan said.

Ben slid into the booth beside me. "I missed you," he said.

Across the table, Morgan made goo-goo eyes at me.

She adored Ben. She especially adored the fact that his family was extremely well off, and that he went to the most exclusive private school in the city, and — perhaps most importantly — that he wasn't Nick, whom she claimed to like (*"Really,* Robyn, you know I do"). But the last time she'd compared Ben and Nick, she'd said, "You have to be realistic, Robyn. Ben is looking at a future with serious money while Nick is probably looking at serious time in a correctional facility." I'd given her a sharp look, even though it was true that Nick had been in trouble with the law. But that was all in the past — at least, I hoped it was. "No offence to Nick," Morgan had said. "I think he's cute and everything, but, come on, Robyn, Ben has it all."

She was right. He did.

And I liked him. I really did.

But every time my phone rang, during those few seconds it took to lift it to my ear, I always hoped — *prayed* — that the voice on the other end would be Nick's.

It never was.

Nick had vanished at the beginning of December while I was out of town on a school trip. I had no idea where he was or why he had left. He'd sent me a Christmas present — without a return address. He'd been gone for six weeks so far and hadn't called even once. By now I was supposed to have put him behind me — according to Morgan and my mother. On good days, I agreed with them and got angry all over again about the inconsiderate way he had treated me. I even told myself that I was better off without him. On so-so days, I managed to half-convince myself that I didn't care about him anymore — why should I? He obviously didn't care about me. But on most days, like now, I missed him.

You're doing it again, I told myself sternly. You're being stupid. You're not facing facts. Nick took off. Nick didn't care enough to even leave a note. Nick hasn't called. Nick isn't here.

But Ben is.

Ben was sitting beside me with an arm around me, smiling at me, and telling me that he had missed me.

"I missed you, too," I said.

He beamed as if I had just handed him a winning lottery ticket. Ben always made me feel like there was no one he'd rather be with than me.

"You want to do something this weekend?" he said.

"Like?"

"I was thinking hiking."

Morgan stared at him. "It's *January*," she said.

Ben looked pleasantly across the table at her, waiting for her to make her point.

"In January, people ski," Morgan said. "Or they skate. Or snowshoe. They do not hike."

"What's this about hiking?" said someone else. It was Billy. "Is someone going hiking?"

Morgan started out by giving him her sternest and most unforgiving look — punishing him for the puppy-dog expression he'd had on his face during Ms Denholm's class — but she yielded fast when he squeezed into the booth beside her. He slipped an arm around her, and she sighed and nestled close. She looked starry-eyed and content. Anyone who first met Morgan when she was painted onto Billy would totally get the wrong idea of what she was really like.

"I'm taking Robyn hiking up in Limestone Valley," Ben said. "You know it?" Billy nodded. "You ever hiked it in winter?" Billy shook his head, but he looked interested. Morgan must have noticed.

"Well, don't get any ideas," she said. "We already have plans for the weekend." They were volunteering together for Morgan's favourite cause — the fashion industry's gala to raise money for breast cancer research. Morgan loved it because it let her get up close and personal with some high-profile people in the fashion business and — I suspect — because as assistant head of the table decorating committee, she got to boss people around. Billy was tagging along because he adored Morgan and because, as Morgan never tired of pointing out, fair was fair. Morgan had spent last Saturday with Billy at an animal rescue shelter where Billy helped out a couple of times a month.

"Besides, I'm sure Robyn and Ben want to be alone," Morgan said.

Ben grinned and held me tight. I snuggled close to him and pushed away my memories of how it used to feel when Nick held me.

Chapter 3

"Are you sure this is a good idea?" I said to, of all people, my mother. Anyone who knows my mother knows that she is immensely practical and level-headed. She has a Type-A personality and is the kind of person who not only plans but *over*-plans every detail of her life. Who leaves nothing to chance. Who advertises far and wide that she does *not* like surprises. Who was going out with a financial analyst — another type of person who neither likes nor appreciates surprises.

"Of course it's a good idea," my mother said. "Ted has been under a lot of pressure." Ted Gold was the financial analyst my mother was seeing. He had recently asked her to marry him. She hadn't said yes, but she hadn't said no, either. We were on our way to his condo. "I think he's been working too hard," my mother said. "He hasn't taken a single day off since Christmas. He needs something to brighten his week."

"If you want to surprise Ted with a gourmet indoor picnic in January, that's fine with me, Mom. But why do I have to be there? The last time I checked, three was a crowd."

"Ted thinks of you as the daughter he never had. He adores you, Robyn. You always make him laugh. I thought if we could have a sort of family evening — "

I stared at her.

"A *family* evening?" That didn't sound remotely like my mother. Unless: "Are you finally going to give Ted an answer?" It was the only explanation I could think —

Uh-oh. Wait a minute.

"Or are you afraid that he's going to insist on an answer?" I said, suspicious now. "Is that why you made me come — because you think he won't say anything if I'm there?"

My mother flushed as she hit the turn signal and made a left into the driveway that led to the under-ground parking garage at Ted's building.

"Which is it, Mom?"

She slowed the car to a stop, pressed the button to lower the driver's side window, reached out, and punched some numbers into the keypad that controlled the garage door to the visitors' parking area. The door began to open.

"Mom?"

She glanced at me and sighed. "I know Ted wants an answer," she said. "I know he's not going to wait forever. But we've been seeing each other for less than a year. That isn't very long."

"You told me you only went out with Dad for three months before he asked you to marry him."

"Exactly," my mother said. "Act in haste, repent at leisure. I need more time, Robyn. This is a big decision. But if I say that to Ted . . . " Her voice trailed off, but I knew what she meant. She had already told him once that she needed more time. If she told him again, he might not understand. Or he might get impatient. I guess it meant something that she wanted to avoid that.

We were silent as she eased the car into the visitors' parking area and started to hunt for a space.

"There's one," she said triumphantly. As she nudged the car deeper into the garage, I glanced out the passenger-side window and started in surprise. Was that . . . ? No, it couldn't be. I must be seeing things.

I twisted in my seat to take another look, but it was too late. My mother had manoeuvred the car into a parking space near the elevator. Satisfied, she pulled her keys from the ignition, got out, and circled around to the trunk. I jumped out and headed back in the direction we had come to see if my eyes had been playing tricks on me.

"Oh no you don't," my mother said. "You're not bailing out on me. Come on. Help me with this."

This was a store-packed wicker hamper that contained smoked salmon, pâté, sliced meats, two different kinds of salad, two different kinds of bread, and an assortment of raw veggies and condiments. (I'd peeked.) Also in the trunk of the car was a bottle of wine with a bow tied around its neck, a bouquet of fresh-cut flowers, and a bakery box. I took the wine, the flowers, and the bakery box, and left my mother to tote the hamper. We took the parking-garage elevator as far as it would go, which from the visitors' parking area was only one floor, up to the lobby. Ted lives in a secure building — all visitors have to pass the front desk and sign in. The security guard's normally stern face softened when he recognized my mother.

"Ms Stone," he said. "Good to see you again. Do you want me to ring him?"

My mother shook her head.

"It's a surprise, Darren," she said.

Darren grinned as he noted the hamper, the flowers, the wine bottle, and the bakery box.

We crossed the lobby to the main elevators and rode up to Ted's super-luxurious penthouse condominium. When we got out of the elevator, my mother insisted that we approach Ted's door stealthily, like a couple of burglars. Before she rang the doorbell, she whispered to me to stand out of view of the peephole.

"But if he can't see who's out here, he won't open the door," I whispered back.

"He shouldn't," my mother said. "But he will." I wondered how she knew that. Had she surprised Ted before? "He insists that because this is a secure building, anyone who rings his doorbell must be a neighbour."

My mother was right. Within seconds, Ted swung the door open and my mother did something that I'd never seen her do before. She leaped in front of the open door like a schoolgirl and yelled, "Surprise!"

Ted froze. He stared at my mother in stunned silence. From somewhere behind Ted, I heard an all-too-familiar voice say, "Well, Patti. This *is* a surprise."

Well, that answered *that* question. I'd caught the last few numbers on the licence plate on the black Porsche I'd seen in the visitors' parking area. Now I knew what the rest of them were — it had been my father's car.

Ted turned slowly and looked mournfully at my father, who had appeared in the doorway behind him. My father gave a nothing-you-can-do-about-it-now shrug. My mother's smile evaporated.

"What are you doing here, Mac?" she said before turning to Ted and demanding. "What is he doing here?"

"Uh," Ted said. "Uh . . . "

My father looked at the picnic hamper that my mother was carrying and at the flowers, wine, and bakery box that I was holding.

"As a matter of fact," he said smoothly, "I was just leaving." He squeezed past Ted, either ignoring or oblivious to the venomous look in my mother's eyes. "I'll wait downstairs for a few minutes," he whispered as he passed me. "Just in case."

My mother watched him walk to the elevator and press the Down button. She waited, holding the picnic hamper with white-knuckled hands, until the elevator arrived and he stepped inside. As soon as the doors slid shut, she turned to Ted and said, "What's going on?"

"Nothing," Ted said. His eyes skipped away from her, and his ears turned red. He was the worst liar I had ever seen.

"Let me put it another way," my mother said, speaking slowly now, the way she does when she's trying to keep her temper leashed and avoid confusion by being as precise as possible with her questions, the way lawyers (like my mother) do when they're cross-examining a hostile or uncooperative witness. "What possible reason could you have for meeting with my ex-husband?"

I guess that Ted hadn't had much experience with my mother's super-tough lawyer voice because he seemed startled by it and, instead of just answering the question, he attempted evasive manoeuvres.

"How do you know he didn't just drop by?" he said.

"Mac? Why would he *just drop by?*" my mother said, as if the notion of my father appearing on a whim were as absurd as a giraffe suddenly dropping into her bathtub — which it was. Her eyes narrowed. "Does this have anything to do with me? Because if it does — "

She didn't finish her sentence. She didn't have to. Ted and I both knew what she meant: if my father's presence had anything at all to do with my mother, Ted was going to be picnicking alone — forever. If there was one thing that my mother refused to tolerate, it was my father interfering in any way in her personal life.

"No," Ted said. "Your name didn't even come up. I swear."

My mother stared at him as if she were trying to read him the way she might read a witness for the prosecution. Finally she said, "He didn't just drop by, did he, Ted?"

Ted shook his head. "I asked him to come over."

"Why?"

Ted peered at my mother through the thick lenses of his gold-rimmed glasses. "It's a personal matter."

My mother stiffened. "Personal? You invited *my* ex-husband over without telling me, and now you're saying it's *personal?*"

Ted held his ground — reluctantly, if you ask me. He glanced at me. I think that's when my mother remembered that I was still there.

"Robyn, I need to speak to Ted alone."

"Maybe I can catch up with Dad," I said. She didn't answer. Nor did she look at me. Neither of them did.

"Patricia," Ted said, "all I'm asking is that you respect my privacy."

"And all *I'm* asking," my mother said, thrusting the hamper at him, "is that you tell me what my ex-husband was doing here."

They locked eyes like two schoolyard bullies, neither one wanting to back down. I handed my mother the flowers, the wine, and the bakery box, and hurried to the elevator. I found my father in the lobby, leaning casually against the security desk, engaged in conversation with Darren, the security guard. He did not look surprised to see me.

"Has your mother calmed down?" he said.

"I don't think so. But you're driving me home."

My father pushed himself away from the desk. "My pleasure, Robbie," he said.

It wasn't until I was fastening my seat belt in my father's Porsche that I asked, "What were you doing at Ted's anyway?"

My father turned the key in the ignition and put the car into reverse.

"I can't tell you that, Robbie."

"Why not? It's not like he's a client." My father runs his own private security company and does very well at it. But he has a rule: he *never* talks about his clients — well, other than to boast occasionally about the famous ones.

He didn't look at me. He shifted gears and steered the car toward the exit while I absorbed his silence.

"Wait a minute," I said. "You mean that Ted *is* a client?" That had to be it. "Why did he hire you?"

My father slowed the car as he reached the exit to the garage.

"You know I can't discuss my business with you," he said.

So I was right. Ted *was* a client. But no matter how hard I tried and how many times I swore myself to secrecy, my father refused to tell me anything, which left me wondering why someone like Ted would hire someone like my father. The only thing I knew for sure was that Ted must have a problem — and that it must be a big one.

My mother's car was already in the driveway when

my father pulled up at the curb, which told me (a) that she and Ted hadn't had much of a conversation after I left and (b) that she must have broken the speed limit getting home. She tends to drive aggressively when she's angry. I saw her standing in the foyer, peering out the window. She opened the front door when she saw us.

"I love you, Robbie," my father said. "But do me a favour and get out of the car right now."

I glanced up at the house. My mother was outside now. She had a coat over her shoulders and had started down the front steps.

"Please, Robbie?" my father said.

I opened the passenger door. "You owe me one, Dad."

"Any time."

When my mother saw me get out of the car, she started to jog down the front walk.

"Mac!" she called.

My father reached across the front seat and pulled the passenger door shut. He was roaring down the street before my mother was halfway to the curb. She muttered something under her breath — I think it had to do with men — shivered, and stomped back up the walk to the house.

Chapter 4

Ben was at my house bright and early the next morning. My mother, who may or may not still have been thinking unkind thoughts about the male of the species, greeted him warmly at the door. Like Morgan, she adored Ben, and for a lot of the same reasons, except that to my mother, Ben's number-one attraction was that he wasn't Nick. In other words, Ben had never been arrested, had never been charged with a crime, had never been convicted, and had never served time in a correctional facility. She didn't even seem to notice, let alone mind, when Ben slipped an arm around my waist and planted a kiss on my cheek right in front of her.

"I'll have her home by six, Ms Stone," he said.

"And, of course, you'll stay for supper," my mother said, beaming at him.

A few moments later, while I was buckling my seat belt, Ben said, "Your mother is really nice."

She is — when she wants to be. But I couldn't help

23

thinking that she had never invited Nick to supper.

We drove out of the city, heading north. The farther we went, the larger the spaces grew between the houses until, finally, we were looking at farmhouses surrounded by fields and pastures.

"I keep forgetting that everything isn't concrete and high-rises," I said, gazing at the rolling hills and snow-covered fields.

"I come out here to hike all the time," Ben said.

"Define 'all the time.' "

"As often as I can. Winter, spring, summer, and fall — it's completely different every season, and it's always beautiful."

When Ben finally pulled the car off the road, it felt as if we were the only two people in the world. There were no houses in sight, no other cars whizzed past us, and no other hikers were visible in any direction.

"If you come out here at any other time of year, you always run into lots of people," Ben said. "But in winter, people either head for the ski hills or they stay home. It's so peaceful."

We pulled on hats and mitts, wound scarves around our necks, and shouldered backpacks packed with thermoses of hot tea, sandwiches, fruit, and bottles of water. Then, bundled against the elements, we set off up a snow-covered hiking trail. Ben took the lead. I climbed behind him, breathing in the crisp country air. We hiked for nearly an hour, mostly uphill, before Ben stopped and smiled at me.

"Put out your hand," he said.

"Why?"

"Trust me."

I stuck out my right hand. Ben turned it gently so that it was palm up. He pulled off my mitten.

"Hey," I said. The cold air nipped my fingers.

"You could do it with your mitts on, but it's better bare-handed," he said.

"Do what?"

He dug into his pocket and pulled out a small bag.

"What is that?" I said. "Birdseed?"

He nodded and poured some into my upturned hand.

"Do I throw it?"

"No. Just keep your hand out like this." He demonstrated. "It won't take long."

Ben was right. Less than a minute had passed before a grey-and-white ball of fluff with bright black eyes flitted through the air toward me and landed on my outstretched hand. It was a chickadee so small that it was almost weightless. Its tiny toes gently pinched my finger, its little head bobbed down, it snatched up a seed, and then, *poof*, it was gone.

"Wait," Ben said when I started to lower my hand.

A moment later, another tiny chickadee landed. Then another and another. Sometimes there were two little fluffballs pecking at the seeds in my hand. At other times, one bird landed as soon as another had taken off. Ben watched me, smiling, until the last seed was gone.

"Want more?" he said.

I shook my head. "My hand is numb."

Ben slipped my mitt back on for me and massaged

my hand gently until it warmed up.

"Come on," he said. "I want to show you a special place."

We walked until we came to an enormous, dense growth of mature cedar trees. The rich green of the foliage and the rust colour of the bark stood out sharply against the pristine white of the snow. I breathed deeply, inhaling the cedary perfume.

"Smells great, doesn't it?" Ben said. He slipped his arms around me and pulled me close. "Kind of romantic, don't you think?"

I smiled and looked up into his green eyes. He pulled me even closer and kissed me.

I liked Ben. I liked when he kissed me. I liked when he held me. I liked that Morgan and my mother both liked him. But . . .

"You're the best thing that's ever happened to me," he murmured.

I pulled back a little. "What do you mean?"

"I mean I like seeing you. I like being with you. I like thinking about being with you. The best days, Robyn, are the days when I know we're going to be together." He wrapped his arms around me and pulled me close again. I let him. That way, he couldn't see the expression on my face. I liked Ben, and I liked being with him. But I was starting to get the feeling that he was more serious about me than I was about him.

He held me a little longer. Then he said, "Come on. Wait until you see the spot I picked out for lunch."

I followed him up the trail.

The sun shone in a cloudless sky overhead, making the snow-covered terrain sparkle. My breath hung in white puffs in front of my face, but it didn't feel cold as I trudged up a hill and along a ridge behind Ben. Every now and then he turned and smiled at me, and I smiled back and reminded myself how sweet and nice he was, sort of like Billy. He cared about other people. He volunteered at a drop-in shelter for the homeless where he knew most of the clients and treated them just like anyone else, even though he himself was as privileged as they were under-privileged. I reminded myself, too, that Nick had walked out on me without a word of explanation and that Ben would never do anything like that.

"Well?" Ben said finally. "What do you think?"

We had been climbing steadily, but I had kept my eyes down most of the way, watching the uneven terrain, judging where to step, mindful of the rocks and tree roots that lay buried beneath the snow and that had already tripped me up a couple of times. I was breathing hard, too. I'm in pretty good shape, but I couldn't remember the last time I'd taken a long — a very long — uphill hike.

I came to a stop beside Ben and looked around.

"Wow," I said.

Ben broke into a blissful smile. "Beautiful, isn't it?"

What an understatement! We were standing at the edge of a high ridge from which we could see over the tops of pines, spruces, and skeletal birches to a frozen lake beyond. A long, narrow piece of rock jutted out like a huge finger over the landscape far below. Ben walked to the end of it and gazed around. I stayed where I was, on much more solid ground. I liked the view but I don't like heights, especially when they feature sharp drop-offs. But even from where I stood, I had a perfect view of the lake and of the land that rose around it, which was studded with more pines, spruces, birches, and firs. There wasn't another human being in sight.

"It really is nice," I said.

Ben was standing at the edge of the finger of rock now. It made me queasy to look at him. Then, without looking down, he stretched out his arms and threw back his head. Slowly at first, and then faster, he began to spin out there on the edge of the earth.

"Ben! Ben, be careful."

He whirled and whirled, his feet dancing him around faster and faster.

"Ben!" My heart was in my throat. Was he crazy? What if he got dizzy? What if he fell?

Then it happened. One of his feet slipped off the edge.

"Help!" he shouted.

His eyes grew wide and his hands pinwheeled frantically in the air as he scrabbled for something to grab onto. But there was nothing — nothing but air.

I lunged forward and grabbed at his jacket. My hand closed around the top of it, near the collar, and I yanked him toward me. I was terrified to look down. At first I was afraid that he was going to pull me over with him. But he didn't.

"What are you doing?" I said, relieved and angry

and scared all at the same time. "You could have killed yourself."

He looked at me and tugged me toward him. I resisted. My heart was pounding, and I was angry with him for spinning around out there in the first place. He should have known better than to take such a chance. But he was stronger than I was and, despite my resistance, I found myself pressed against the front of his parka. He wrapped his arms around me. I was breathing hard. My heart was still racing, but I didn't dare struggle. We were still out there at the end of the finger of rock. I didn't want him to fall. I didn't want to fall.

Ben started to tremble. At least, that's what I thought he was doing until I looked up at his face. He wasn't trembling at all. He was laughing.

"You think this is *funny?*" I said. "You scared me, Ben. I thought you were going to fall." I tried to struggle out of his grip, but he held me tightly.

"I was just checking to see if you cared," he said, grinning at me, his body shaking with suppressed laughter.

"By risking your *life?*" I said. Boy, was I mad.

"Look down, Robyn."

"What?"

"Look down. Please."

I clung to him as I peeked below. When I did, I felt like pushing him over the edge — not that it would have had much impact. Less than a metre below the finger of rock that he had been spinning on, but completely invisible from where I had been standing, a thick, snow-covered ledge jutted out. If Ben had slipped off the rock, he would have had a close and soft landing. He wouldn't have even bruised himself, but he would have scared me to death.

"See?" he said. "I was perfectly safe. I've done a joke fall off here at least a dozen times. You should have seen the look on my buddy Alan's face the first time I tried it." He laughed again.

"But I thought — " I stared at his grinning face.

"I'm sorry," he said, still chuckling. "But if you'd seen your expression . . . And you do care, don't you?"

"I didn't want anything bad to happen to you." I looked into his mischievous eyes. "But now I'm not so sure."

"I won't do it again," he said. "I promise. Are you hungry? There's a hikers' shelter just up the trail."

We made our way to a three-sided wooden hut that had benches along the walls and that offered a spectacular view of the lake below. Ben opened our packs, laid out the food we had brought, and handed me a sandwich. I was surprised at how hungry I was. I devoured that sandwich and reached for another one. Ben poured hot sugary tea for both of us and leaned back against the wall while he drank it.

After we ate, we hiked partway around the lake. Ben stayed close to me now and talked the whole way about the history of the area. It had once been filled with forests and logging camps, he said, but those had gradually given way to farms and farmers' fields — the rolling countryside was still dotted with barns and farmhouses and marked off with fences and rows of trees that served as windbreaks to protect the fields. Now, slowly but surely, the farmers were selling their land to developers, and subdivisions were springing up where cows had grazed and corn had grown.

Finally we went back to the car and started for home.

"I've been thinking," Ben said. "We have a place up north. My father calls it a cottage, but it's not really. It's more like a country house. I thought we could go up there for March break."

We? "You and me?"

"Any other time, Peter would probably insist that he or Catherine be there to chaperone." Peter is Ben's father. Catherine is his wife. "But the baby is due any time now, so that won't be a problem. I already invited Morgan and Billy to come with us."

"You did?"

"Morgan said yes. She seems really excited about the idea. So how about it? We can spend the whole week together. And we can start making plans for the summer."

Summer? It was only January.

"I was thinking we could do something with Habitat for Humanity. They need volunteers all over the world. I was thinking South America. Or there's another organization I heard about — it builds schools in poor villages and neighbourhoods. I put our names down for an information session so that we can find out more about it."

"You what?" I wasn't following everything he was

saying. He was moving too fast.

"We don't have to make a decision right away," he said. "We'll just see what's involved. We can do something useful for a month or so. Then we can travel for a couple of weeks before coming home. It'll be a real adventure."

"Well, I — "

He flashed me a smile. "We'll have a great time, Robyn," he said. "I know we will."

"But — "

"Can you think of a better way to spend the summer than by building a school in a little village in, say, the mountains of Peru — or maybe somewhere in the rainforest in Brazil?"

I had to admit that I couldn't.

"What do you say? You want to do it?"

A whole week together at March break? Two months together during the summer?

"We'll see," I said. I like Ben. The fact that he was thinking of spending his summer as a volunteer proves what a nice guy he is. But, "I need to think about it." As the words came out of my mouth, I realized that I sounded exactly like my mother.

"Morgan already said yes," Ben said. He sounded disappointed.

"I need to think about it, Ben," I said again.

I knew I hadn't reacted the way he had hoped, but I didn't want to commit to anything until I was sure it was what I wanted. Ben slipped a CD into the car's sound system, and we listened in silence all the way home. When he finally pulled to a stop in front of my house and I unbuckled my seat belt and opened the passenger-side door, he didn't move.

"My mom invited you for supper, remember?" I said.

"Apologize to her for me, will you?"

"Are you mad at me?" I said.

"No," he said, but I didn't believe him. "But it's been a long day. I'm tired."

"You *are* mad at me," I said.

He shook his head. "I'm not. Really. I'll call you tomorrow, okay?"

I said okay. I said my mother would be disappointed. But, secretly, I was relieved. Things were moving too fast. *Ben* was moving too fast. He was expecting too much.

* * *

"Where's Ben?" my mother said when I went into the house. "I thought he was going to have supper with us."

"He said to tell you he's sorry. He's tired. So am I. We hiked all day."

"But I made lemon chicken," she said.

Lemon chicken is my mother's company dish. She makes it whenever she invites someone to dinner for the first time. It's relatively easy to prepare, completely foolproof, and utterly delicious. People never fail to compliment her lavishly or to ask for seconds. My mother had obviously been hoping to make a good impression on Ben. That's why I decided not to tell her about his March break invitation. She would probably think it was a good idea.

"He doesn't know what he's missing," I said. "But to tell you the truth, Mom, I could probably eat the whole thing myself."

"Good," my mother said. "Because I made enough to feed both of us and one teenaged boy. Go and get changed. I'll start the salad."

I ran upstairs and, hurried along by the aroma of the chicken, quickly changed out of my flannel-lined jeans, long underwear, and thick socks. I was on the way back downstairs when I heard the doorbell. I groaned. I wanted to eat now. I didn't want to be delayed by an unexpected visitor.

"Get that, will you, Robyn?" my mother called to me from the kitchen.

I veered for the front door and opened it.

It was Ted. He smiled nervously at me.

"Is your mother home?" he said.

In fact, she had come out of the kitchen and was standing right behind me, a serving spoon in one hand and salad tongs in the other. "Ted," she said. Her tone was as frosty as the night air.

"Patricia. I need to talk to you. To both of you."

My mother stared at him a little longer. Her eyes were cold and hard. Boy, I knew what that was all about. She used to have the same look on her face whenever my father showed up for supper four or five hours late, or when he got called away in the middle of an anniversary celebration or, a couple of times, during Christmas dinner. She sounded far from friendly when she said, "Come in." But at least she said it.

I stepped aside to let Ted pass. He unbuttoned his overcoat and slowly peeled it off, but instead of hanging it in the closet the way he usually did when he breezed into the house with my mother, he stood in the front hall with it in his arms, as if he were a stranger. And my mother said, "Robyn, take Ted's coat," as if this were his first visit to our home instead of his hundredth.

"We were just about to eat supper," she said as I reached for Ted's coat. Instead of releasing it, he pulled it away from me.

"I didn't mean to interrupt," he said. "I just wanted to talk to you — about last night. I'm sorry I upset you, Patricia."

My mother loves to hear the words *I'm sorry*. She claims never to have heard them from my father. Her face softened slightly. She handed me the serving spoon and the salad tongs. "Take these into the dining room," she said to me. She gently tugged Ted's coat out of his hands, and hung it in the closet.

"I'm assuming you haven't eaten yet," she said to Ted.

"I have to tell you something first, Patricia." He glanced at me. "Both of you."

My mother nudged him into the living room and made him sit on the sofa. She sat beside him, not as close as she did when she was in the mood to snuggle, but not at the far end of the sofa, either.

I sank into an armchair opposite them.

Ted peered into my mother's eyes, drew in a deep breath, and said, "Mac was at my place last night because I hired him about a month ago to do some work for me."

My mother looked confused. She was probably trying to figure out what work my father, a former police officer, could possibly be doing for Ted, a mild-mannered, law-abiding financial analyst.

"You're a client of Mac's?" she said. "What's wrong? Are you in trouble, Ted? Has someone threatened you?"

"No," Ted said quickly. "Nothing like that. I hired him to . . . find someone for me."

The private security business, as defined by my father, isn't all or even mostly about security per se. My father also does investigations — all kinds of investigations, for all kinds of people, including lawyers, insurance companies, other kinds of companies, and individuals.

"Who did you ask him to find?" my mother said.

Ted looked away.

"Ted?"

"My daughter," Ted said quietly.

"You have a *daughter?*" I said.

My mother looked sharply at me. But when she turned back to Ted, she said the same thing I had just said. "You have a daughter?" Her tone was much gentler than mine, but it was obvious that this was news to her, too.

"I was going to tell you. I was going to tell you a dozen times. But it's one of those things that the longer you put it off, the harder it becomes to talk about it."

"I don't understand," my mother said. "What's so hard about saying that you have a daughter?" An answer must have occurred to her because she suddenly said, "Oh." She looked sympathetically at Ted. "I would never judge you, Ted," she said.

Ted squirmed in his seat. "It's not what you're probably thinking," he said. He looked at her as if she were a bed of hot coals that he was now going to attempt to cross in his bare feet. "I was married. To the girl's mother."

"Oh," my mother said again. The stunned look on her face told me that this was also news to her.

"I sort of have a tendency not to mention it," Ted said.

My mother was silent. She seemed paralysed.

"I wasn't trying to hide it from you," Ted said. "I swear I wasn't."

Even I had trouble believing that. There are some things that aren't important to mention, like how poorly you did on your eighth-grade math finals or that you were still taking a favourite blanket to bed with you long after preschool. Things like that don't matter. They're trivial. But there are other things, bigger things, that do matter. If you make a point of not mentioning those things, no matter what you say or what excuse you offer, people are naturally going to assume that you are hiding them. Proposing marriage to someone without telling her that you've been married before and have a daughter was one of those things.

"You were married?" my mother said finally. She

seemed to be having trouble believing this. "And you never mentioned it? All those times I was trying to explain — " She glanced at me. "All those times we talked about what can go wrong between two people, why didn't you tell me?"

Ted wriggled as if his suit had suddenly shrunk two sizes and was strangling him. "I was embarrassed," he said.

"Embarrassed?" my mother said. "You know practically everything there is to know about my marr — " She glanced at me again. She was probably wishing I wasn't there. "What could you possibly be embarrassed about?"

Ted shook his head. He tried to take my mother's hands in his, but she pulled them away.

"You've heard what people say about some of those celebrity marriages," he said. "You know, that they last all of five minutes. Well, my marriage was like that."

"You were married to a celebrity?" I said. Way to go, Ted!

My mother gave me an exasperated look.

"No," Ted said. "But I was married for about five minutes. I think about it sometimes and I still can't figure out what was going through my mind when I proposed. Or what was going through Beth's when she accepted."

"Beth was your wife?" my mother said. It was hard to tell what she was thinking.

"Beth was the woman I married, yes," Ted said carefully, as if he were clarifying the matter. I didn't see the distinction, but he obviously did and it was obviously important to him.

"I see," my mother said, but it was clear to me, if not to Ted, that she didn't. "You were married for five minutes — "

"Actually, it was more like six months," Ted said.

" — to someone named Beth, and you managed to produce a daughter in that space of time?"

"The reason we got married was because Beth was pregnant," Ted said. His cheeks turned pink. "I was the father and I guess I thought marriage was the right thing to do. But Beth and I weren't compatible. Not even remotely. One day while I was at work, she packed her bags and left. She took Bonnie with her."

"Bonnie?" my mother said. "Your daughter?"

Ted nodded. "She didn't tell me where she was going. I contacted all of her friends. No one would tell me anything. They all claimed they didn't know, but I think Beth told them not to speak to me. So I waited for her to contact me. I figured she would, you know, for child support." He blinked at my mother from behind his gold-framed glasses. "But she never did." He sounded as if he still couldn't believe it. "She never called. Never wrote. Nothing." Boy, did I know what that felt like! "Finally I hired someone to track her down. She didn't like that. She said she never wanted to see me again and she didn't consider me part of Bonnie's life. She said I was the biggest mistake she had ever made. Then she filed for divorce."

My mother reached out and took Ted's hands in hers.

"I'm sorry, Ted," she said.

"I had to go to court to get visiting rights," Ted said. "Beth didn't like that, either. She was living with someone else by then and she made it clear, through her lawyer, that she didn't appreciate me 'interfering,' as she put it. She told me the new man in her life didn't like it, either. But Bonnie was my daughter."

He kept using that word, *was*.

"Bonnie was five by the time I won the right to see her. It wasn't easy, though. Because of the distance, I couldn't arrange to see her every week or even every other weekend, the way some divorced fathers do." The way my father did. "Instead, I was supposed to get her for a week at Christmas and for two weeks in the summer. But even that didn't work out."

"What do you mean?" my mother said.

"Beth always called with a problem. She said that Bonnie was sick. Or that she had been invited to a friend's place and that she'd be devastated if she couldn't go. Once I went to meet the plane that Bonnie was supposed to be on, but she wasn't there. I almost had a heart attack. I thought someone had taken her. It turned out that Beth had changed her mind at the last minute and hadn't sent her. She didn't bother to let me know." He drew in a deep breath. "The year Bonnie was going to turn eight, I drove all the way out to where she was living to get her. Beth was furious with me. I was supposed to have Bonnie for two weeks. It was a terrible visit. Bonnie cried herself to sleep every night. She said she missed Beth and was afraid of what would happen to her if she wasn't there."

"What you do mean, afraid?" my mother said.

"I don't know. But she kept telling me she wanted to go home, that she didn't want to be with me in the first place, and that she'd only come because her mother had insisted. That's when I realized that it hadn't been all Beth's fault. She'd tried, but my daughter didn't want to be with me. She didn't want anything to do with me."

"She was just a child," my mother said.

"I know. I mean, I know *now*. But at the time . . . " He shrugged helplessly. "I didn't know anything about being a father. And I sure didn't *feel* like a father. After a week of her being completely miserable, I put her on a plane back home. Then . . . " He hung his head.

"Then what?" my mother said gently.

"Beth's lawyer contacted me. Beth wanted permission for her second husband to adopt Bonnie. And I . . . " He shook his head. "I gave it," he said. "I let her go, Patricia. I let it all go — my five minutes of marriage and of being a father. I pretended that none of it had ever happened."

"Ted . . . "

"I'm so ashamed of myself. It was three years before I picked up the phone to call Beth again to see how Bonnie was. By then, the number I had for her was out of service. I flew out to where she lived, but she had moved. She'd quit her job, too. One of her co-workers told me that she'd broken up with her second husband

and that she'd left town. She didn't tell anyone where she was going. At least, that's what this co-worker said. I asked around some more. I talked to dozens of people. But I couldn't find anyone who knew — or who would tell me — anything. So I let it go again. Up until a few months ago, I thought I could let it go for good. I thought I could just forget about it."

"I still don't understand why didn't you tell me," my mother said.

Ted looked at her, his eyes glistening. "Are you kidding? A guy like me? Look at me. I'm not great-looking, I'm as blind as a bat without my glasses, I'm almost completely bald. How would you have reacted if, in addition to all that, I'd told you that my wife had dumped me after the shortest marriage on record and that my only child hates me? You would never have gone out with me."

"Ted, you are the nicest, sweetest, most considerate and dependable man that I have ever met . . . "

He looked gratefully at her. "I should have told you, Patricia. But when I first met you . . . I was trying to make a *good* impression, not come across as a pathetic divorced dad whose daughter hates him so much that she never wants to see him. And after what you'd been through — " Both of them turned and looked at me this time, afraid, I think, of seeming to criticize my father in front of me. I sighed. I love my father, no matter what my mother thinks of him. I see him regularly. He'll always be part of my life and I couldn't imagine anything that my mother or Ted could say that would change that. "I wanted you to like me."

"I do like you."

"I mean, I wanted to make a favourable first impression. A very favourable first impression."

My mother smiled gently and squeezed his hand.

"After that . . . " He shrugged. "I couldn't think of a good time or a good way to bring it up. What was I supposed to say, Patricia? *Oh, by the way, there's something I've been meaning to tell you . . . "*

"I'm glad you told me now," my mother said. "But what made you decide to try to find her after all these years?"

Ted nodded at me. "Robyn is partly responsible."

"Me?" I said. "What did *I* do?"

"We get along pretty well, don't we?"

I nodded. In fact, Ted and I got along great.

"That made me think that maybe I'd been wrong to give up with Bonnie, that maybe I should have kept on trying. That maybe I could be a good father."

"Ted, you'd be a wonderful father," my mother said.

"You're the other reason I decided to look for her, Patricia. After I asked you to marry me . . . " My mother stiffened slightly. Ted kept hold of her hand and smiled gently at her. "I know you don't feel ready yet. I know you may never feel ready."

"I never said that, Ted."

He looked into her eyes. "But I knew I couldn't marry you unless I was honest about my past. And I knew that I couldn't be honest about it unless I was prepared to confront it and unless I tried to do the right thing — even if it turns out to be too little, too late." He sighed. "But mostly it had to do with me. I have a daughter, Patricia. Maybe she hates me, I don't know. Probably everything she's ever heard about me has been negative. But I'm her father and I at least want the chance to talk to her and to apologize to her for the way I acted. I tried to locate her on my own. I tried everything I could think of — telephone directories, the Internet — but I didn't get anywhere. No Bonnie or Beth Gold. No Bonnie or Beth Fricker — or Duguid."

"Duguid?" my mother said.

"The man she married was named James Duguid," Ted said. "I couldn't locate him, either. So I decided that I needed someone who knew what he was doing. Someone with some expertise in this area."

"So you hired Mac?"

"I asked around. His name kept coming up. And I checked his references. He's very highly regarded."

My mother made no comment.

"Has he found her?" I said.

"No. But he's been looking. And he seems confident that he'll be able to locate her." He turned to my mother. "I'm sorry I didn't tell you sooner, Patricia, and I'm sorry that I was so defensive last night when you saw Mac at my place. I guess I was hoping that I could find Bonnie and see how things went before I told you."

My mother was silent for a few moments. Finally she sighed. "I can't believe I'm saying this," she said, "but if anyone can find her, Mac can. And if that's what you want, then that's what I want, too."

Relief flooded Ted's face.

"Can we have supper now?" I said. My stomach was growling.

Ted tilted his head back and sniffed the air. "Say, do I smell lemon chicken?"

My mother smiled.

* * *

I called Morgan right after supper.

"You're supposed to be my best friend," I said.

"*Supposed* to be?" Morgan said.

"Best friends don't keep secrets from each other, Morgan."

There were a few moments of silence, followed by, "I *am* your best friend, and I'm not keeping anything from you."

Right.

"March break," I said.

There was another pause. She was probably trying to figure out her best defence.

"There's a difference between a secret and a surprise," she said at last. "Ben asked Billy and me if we'd like to spend a week at his place up north. But he said not to tell you. He wanted to surprise you."

"Well, he sure did."

"You don't sound pleasantly surprised. What's the matter? Don't you want to go?"

"I'm not sure."

"What's not to be sure about? You like Ben, don't you?"

"Yes, I guess."

"You guess?"

"He's nice," I said.

"He's totally hot. And he has serious money."

"He's going too fast, Morgan. He wants me to spend the summer with him building a school somewhere in South America."

"It sounds like he likes you a lot," Morgan said.

It sure did.

"Robyn, he's here. He's nice — you just said so yourself. He'd do anything for you. And he'd never hurt you. What's the problem?"

I knew she thought there shouldn't be one. But something about it just didn't feel right to me.

Chapter 5

"You have to come downtown with me," Morgan said after school on Wednesday. "I need someone to share the pain. It's my mom's birthday this weekend and I have to get her a present. Geez, twice a year I go crazy trying to figure out what to buy her — for Christmas and then for her birthday."

"Why don't you just ask her what she wants?" I said.

Morgan rolled her eyes. "You think I don't? Personally, I think if someone asks you what you want for your birthday, you should tell them. It makes life a lot easier and saves you the hassle of having to stand in line to exchange their gift for something you really want. But my mother? Every year I ask her, and every year she says the same thing: Surprise me. Just once I wish she'd surprise me and at least give me a hint. You have to come with me. Two heads are definitely better than one."

"I can't," I said.

"Why not?" she demanded. Then, slowly, a smile spread across her face. "You're meeting Ben, right?"

Ben had called me on Sunday, as promised. He hadn't mentioned March break or the summer. He just wanted to talk and to see how I was doing. He'd called again on Monday. And last night. But: "Wrong. I'm going to the auditions. Ms Denholm made me assistant director of the school play."

"*You're* assistant director?" She made it sound as if I'd just been named next in line for the British throne. "How did *that* happen? What do you know about directing? Come to think of it, what do you even know about drama?"

"Thanks for the vote of confidence."

"I'm sorry," she said. She looked contrite, even if she didn't sound it. "It's just that you've never been involved in a school play before."

True.

"To be honest," I said, "I was surprised when she asked me. I told her that I don't know anything about directing — "

"My point exactly," Morgan said.

"But she said school is a place where you learn. She also said she'd heard good things about me from Ms March."

"Ah," Morgan said. "Now I get it."

"Get what?"

"Why she picked you. Ms March *adores* you because she has a mad crush on your father."

"*What?* Morgan, Ms March is married. She's on *maternity* leave."

"And she was completely bowled over by the famous Mac Hunter charm last term when he came to school to ask about Trisha Carnegie. You said so yourself."

What I had actually said was that Ms March had asked me to stay behind one day and had peppered me with questions about my father. She told me she was thinking of writing a mystery novel while she was on maternity leave. She wanted to know if I thought my father would answer some questions about his experience as a police officer and a private investigator. I said I was sure he would. If there's one thing my father loves, it's regaling people with stories about himself.

"Whatever," I said. "Ms Denholm asked me if I'd do it and I said yes. I have to go to the auditions this afternoon."

"She picked Billy to be set director," Morgan said. She seemed even less pleased by that appointment.

"And you?"

"Me? I'm just a drone. I'm supposed to do what Billy tells me."

"That'll be a nice change," I said. I meant, it would be nice for Billy.

* * *

I was on my way down to the auditorium for the auditions when I passed by Ms Denholm's classroom. The door was open. Ms Denholm was on the far side of the room, looking intently out the window. But there was something odd about the way she was doing it. Instead of standing in front of the window, she had positioned herself sideways between two windows, as if she were trying to make herself invisible to anyone down below. I hesitated. Her personal life was really none of my business. I was just about to continue to the auditorium when she turned around. She gasped when she saw me.

"Robyn," she said breathlessly. "You startled me." She began to move away from the window, but couldn't seem to resist glancing back over her shoulder.

"Is everything okay, Ms Denholm?" I said.

"Of course." She glanced at her watch. "We'd better get going." She turned to the window again, and I don't think I imagined the worried look on her face. I thought about that headless doll nestled among those blood-red roses.

There were two thick binders and two clipboards on her desk. She handed me one of the binders. "This is your copy of the play," she said. "I photocopied it and left lots of space to take notes." Next she handed me a clipboard and a pen. There were half a dozen names and plenty of white space on each of the sheets of paper attached to the clipboard. "These are the students who will be auditioning for parts," she said. "I'd like you to write down any comments you have as you listen to them. I'll do the same. Then I'll have two sets of notes and two opinions to consider when I make the casting decisions."

"What kind of comments do you want me to write?"

"Whatever you think — whether you think the

person should get the part, what you liked and what you didn't like about their audition." She smiled at me. "Don't worry, Robyn. It's not a test. I just want to know what you think."

She picked up the second binder and clipboard and whisked out the door. I scrambled after her. We went down the stairs and across the atrium, where Ms Denholm flung open the doors to the main-floor auditorium.

There were a couple of dozen students inside. Some of them — boys, mostly — were horsing around on the stage, but they stopped when they saw Ms Denholm. Others were sitting or standing quietly near the stage. At first I thought they weren't doing anything. But when I got closer, I saw that a lot of them were mouthing or whispering the lines they had memorized for their audition. Ms Rachlis was on the stage, too, talking to Billy. Billy was in charge of getting the sets done. As art teacher, Ms Rachlis was there to advise him.

Ms Denholm led the way to the front of the auditorium. Everyone settled down to listen as she explained what would happen. She would call out a name. That person would go up on stage and say which role he or she wanted to try out for. Then that person would do the audition piece for that role. If Ms Denholm thought the person might also be good in another role, she would ask him or her to read some dialogue for that role as well. The cast list would be posted as soon as possible.

Billy and Ms Rachlis left the auditorium.

Ms Denholm called out the first name: Rob Stanford. Rob was trying out for the male lead. It turned out that almost all of the boys who were there were trying out for the male lead. (Most of the girls tried out for the female lead.) After Rob had finished, Ms Denholm asked him to read for the part of the police officer in the play. Rob looked surprised, but he did as he was asked. I made a note that he sounded pretty convincing and would probably be good in the part.

Next up was Sam Lee, who turned out to be terrific in the lead. I put a big star next to his name and wrote down that he would be a great lead. Ms Denholm must have liked him, too, because she didn't ask him to read for any other part.

Gordon Cosh was one of the few boys who didn't want the lead role. He wanted to read for the part of the menacing gang leader. He sure looked the part — he was tall and beefy and had a face like a bulldog. But his voice didn't match his appearance. It was high for a boy's voice, and soft.

"That was great, Gordon," Ms Denholm said. "But try to make your voice come from down deep inside, *like this*. And scare us. Be as menacing as you can." She stood up, pulled herself up tall, dropped her voice an octave so that it came out like a rumble, and recited the lines that Gordon had just read. She sounded so much like a tough-guy gang leader that everyone laughed in surprise. A few people applauded when she finished. Ms Denholm smiled and bowed deeply from the waist. "Now you try, Gordon," she said. "I know you can do it."

Gordon didn't look as certain, but he did as he was told. Ms Denholm smiled at the result. Gordon sounded downright scary. I put a star next to his name, too. He was my choice to be the gang leader — unless someone else read for the role and was even more convincing. As it turned out, no one did.

And so it went until, finally, everyone had had a turn. As Ms Denholm explained that she would be reviewing her notes that night and thanked everyone for coming, I turned and saw Billy sitting a few rows behind me, gazing dreamily at Ms Denholm. I got up and slipped into the chair next to his.

"I thought you were meeting with Ms Rachlis," I said.

"I was. But we finished, so I thought I'd stick around and watch the auditions."

"Right," I said, grinning wickedly at him.

Billy's cheeks turned pink, but he didn't say anything.

Kids filed out of the auditorium. Billy and I got up and trailed after them. I got my coat from my locker and then went to meet Billy. By the time I caught up with him, the hallways were deserted. Everyone, even the teachers, had gone home.

As Billy and I headed back down the stairs, we both glanced out the window in the stairwell. I spotted Ms Denholm halfway across the parking lot. She had an enormous purse slung over one shoulder, a bookbag over the other, and her arms filled with books and notebooks — our journals, I bet. We were supposed to write in them every day. She went through them once a week. She stopped beside a small Toyota and set the pile of books and notebooks on the roof of the car while she unlocked and opened the rear door. Her purse slipped off her shoulder. She picked it up and slung it onto the roof of the car, too, while she stowed the bookbag and the stack of books in the back of the car. Then she grabbed her purse and climbed in behind the wheel. A moment later, the little Toyota pulled out onto the street and disappeared.

Billy peered out the window, his hands pressed against his face so that he could see better.

"Come on, Billy," I said. "I'm starving, and I'm supposed to meet my dad for supper." It was turning out to be a late supper. I had already called him once to let him know that the auditions were taking longer than I had expected.

Billy pulled back from the glass. "I think she dropped something," he said.

I glanced outside. "I don't see anything."

Billy started to move again, hurrying down the stairs now.

"I saw something fall out of her purse," he said. "I'm sure of it."

I sighed and went after him. The front door of the school clicked shut behind me.

Sure enough, there was a wallet lying on the ground near where Ms Denholm's car had been parked.

"I told you so," Billy said. He picked it up and handed it to me.

"What are you giving it to *me* for?"

"So you can see if there's a phone number."

"*You* found it," I said, holding it out to him. "You look."

But he refused to take it.

"Okay, fine." I opened it and looked inside. There was some cash, some identification . . . Billy stared at it.

"She's driving without her driver's licence," Billy said, looking over my shoulder. "If she gets pulled over, she'll be in big trouble."

I looked through the whole wallet.

"There's no phone number anywhere in here, Billy. And even if we could get back into the school, what good would it do? There's no one in the office to give us her phone number. We'll just have to wait and give the wallet back to her tomorrow."

"My mom lost her wallet once," Billy said. "She was so afraid it had been stolen that she cancelled all her credit cards and reported all her ID stolen. Then it was a big hassle to get new ones."

I sighed again, dug my cell phone out of a pocket in my backpack, and called directory assistance.

"Well?" Billy said when I finished the call.

"They don't have a listing for her."

"Then we'll have to go to her house," Billy said. I gave him a look. "So she doesn't worry," he said defensively. "I recognize the address on her licence, Robyn. It's not far. She lives right near that new homeless shelter — you know, the one on Selwyn Street."

I knew the place he meant. A lot of people in the neighbourhood had put up a fight when the city had announced that it was being built. They didn't want a bunch of homeless people shuffling around their neighbourhood.

"Since you know where it is, why don't you return it?" I said. I started to hand him the wallet again.

"Come with me."

"Billy, I'm hungry."

"Please, Robyn? You don't want her to worry, do you? Come with me."

Boy, if Morgan could see the way he was acting . . .

I got my phone out again and punched in my father's number. I got his voice mail, so I told him that I'd had a change of plans, that maybe he'd want to go ahead and have supper without me because I had to drop something off at my English teacher's house. Then Billy and I caught the bus.

* * *

"Wow," Billy said when we were finally standing on the sidewalk in front of Ms Denholm's house.

Wow was right. It was a rambling old stone house with two turrets and a wrap-around porch, and it sat on a huge property that was set far back from the road and from its neighbours. Directly opposite it was an enormous and popular park.

I reread the house number and checked it against the address on the driver's licence.

"It's the right place," I said. I started up the walk to the porch. Billy followed me.

I pressed the doorbell and waited.

No one answered.

"Maybe she isn't home yet," Billy said.

"She was driving. We took the bus."

"Maybe she stopped somewhere."

"There are lights on inside, Billy. Someone's home. Maybe the doorbell is broken."

I knocked on the door.

Nothing.

I knocked louder — a lot louder — in case whoever was home was upstairs.

A shadow fell across the door.

A curtain parted.

A face peered out — the face of a very old woman. The door opened.

"Yes?" the woman said in a shaky voice.

"Is Ms Denholm here?" I said.

"What?" the woman said. She bent toward me.

"Ms Denholm," I said, louder this time.

"Who?" the woman said, leaning even closer to me.

"Denholm," I yelled. "We're looking for Ms Denholm."

The old woman's face brightened. "Oh, yes," she said. "Such a nice girl. Around the back."

The back? What did she mean?

"Around the back," the woman said, gesturing this time. "You'll find her around the back."

She closed the door and disappeared inside the cavernous house.

Billy and I left the porch and looked around the side of the house.

"There must be a back entrance," Billy said. He set

off to find it. I followed him around the house and was relieved to see what looked like Ms Denholm's Toyota parked near the back door to the house. Beside the door were two buzzers, but neither was marked.

"Which one?" Billy said.

Good question. I tried the first one. It took a moment, but finally someone said, "Yes?" The voice sounded wary.

"Ms Denholm?" I said.

"Yes?" She sounded even warier.

"It's Robyn and Billy — from school. You dropped your wallet in the school parking lot. We found it — "

There was a long pause. I imagined her checking her purse.

"Come on up," she said at last.

A buzzer sounded. I reached out and pushed the door open. We stepped into a tiny foyer that led immediately to some stairs. I led the way up to a second, much more spacious foyer on the third floor. Ms Denholm was standing in an open doorway on the far side of it.

"I didn't even notice it was gone," she said. "Thank goodness you found it."

"Actually," I said, "it was Billy who spotted it."

She turned and beamed at Billy. "You didn't have to come all the way over here," she said. "You could have waited and returned it tomorrow."

Billy stood there, pink-faced and tongue-tied.

"Billy was afraid you'd worry and start cancelling all your credit cards," I said.

Ms Denholm turned her mega-watt smile on Billy,

whose face went from pink to red. He stared down at the floor.

"Please," Ms Denholm said. "Come in. Let me make you some hot chocolate to warm you up. It's the least I can do."

Billy shuffled uncomfortably.

"Billy is a ve— " I started. Billy nudged me to stop me. Ms Denholm looked quizzically at him.

"You don't like hot chocolate?" she said.

"He doesn't drink cow's milk," I said. "He's a vegan."

"I see," Ms Denholm said. "How about soy milk? I have a carton of it in the fridge."

Billy's face lit up.

"If it's not too much trouble," he said.

"It's no trouble at all. Please, come in."

She stood aside to let us pass. Her apartment was cheerful and roomy. There was a big, bright eat-in kitchen, a spacious living room and dining room with huge windows that looked out over the front of the house and the park across the street. Through a door off a hallway, I caught a glimpse of a large, window-filled bedroom.

"This place is amazing!" I said.

"It is lovely, isn't it?" she said. "I was very lucky to find it. The apartments are brand new. They were put in just last year by the owner's son."

"I think we just met her," I said.

"Mrs. Wyman is in her eighties, and this property must be worth a fortune. Her son says he feels better knowing that there are other people close by, in case anything happens." She took our coats and hung them up along with hers on a couple of pegs inside her front door. "Please, have a seat."

She pulled out a carton of soy milk, a container of cocoa, and a pot to warm the milk. From somewhere below, I heard applause. I glanced at Ms Denholm.

"My landlady is hard of hearing," she said. "When she watches TV, she cranks up the volume. Sometimes she falls asleep with the TV on, and then I have to go downstairs and get her to turn it off. I have a key. Her son — "

Suddenly something thumped on the floor beneath our feet. Billy and I both jumped. Ms Denholm merely sighed.

"That's Mrs. Wyman," she said. "Whenever she needs something or can't find something, she thumps on the ceiling with a broom handle and one of us has to go down and help her. She sometimes calls for help at the least convenient times. But, as I was saying, her son keeps the rent low in exchange for the tenants' agreeing to give her a hand and run errands for her from time to time. I won't be long."

"Mrs. Wyman must be stronger than she looks," Billy said after Ms Denholm had left. "I bet her ceiling is a mess from all that jabbing with a broom handle."

I glanced around. I had never been at a teacher's house before.

"We should go, Billy."

"But she asked us to stay. It would be rude if we just took off."

Ms Denholm's phone rang. I glanced at it. It sat on

a small table in her kitchen with what looked like an old-fashioned answering machine beside it. The phone rang once, twice, three times. After the fourth ring, it fell silent, but the answering machine did not click on. Whoever had called had decided not to leave a message.

Ms Denholm was gone for a full fifteen minutes. Just before she returned, the TV downstairs stopped blaring. She bustled back into the apartment, apologizing profusely for leaving us alone. The milk that she had left on the stove was warm, and she made three mugs of steaming cocoa. She asked Billy how and when he had decided to become a vegan, and the next thing I knew Billy was telling her all about DARC — the Downtown Avian Rescue Club — an organization he had founded. DARC members rescue migrating birds (if they're still alive) that have collided with downtown office towers. They also collect the birds that don't survive these collisions. On most days, the dead outnumber the living. Ms Denholm seemed genuinely interested and asked a lot of questions. Billy was only too delighted to answer.

My stomach rumbled, despite the hot chocolate. I nudged Billy under the table.

"We should get going," I said.

Billy sighed and looked wistfully at Ms Denholm.

"I'll drive you," Ms Denholm said.

"That's okay," I said. "We can take the bus."

Billy shot me a look.

"Nonsense," Ms Denholm said. "You came all this way to return my wallet. And it's cold and dark out there. Just let me wash out these mugs."

She put them into the sink and pulled a heavy, masculine-looking gold ring from the middle finger of her right hand. I must have stared at it because she said, "A lot of people wonder about it — because it's a man's ring."

I didn't want to pry.

"It's a family heirloom," she said. "I had it adjusted to fit my finger. It's very old."

She handed it to me so that I could look at it. It had a flat surface with a crest on it.

"That's the crest of my great-grandmother's family on my father's side," she said.

"It's really heavy."

"And valuable," Ms Denholm said. "Not that I'd ever think of selling it."

She washed the mugs, and Billy muscled me out of the way to grab a dish towel and dry them. Then we all put on our coats and boots and went down the stairs and out the door at the rear of the house where Ms Denholm's car was parked.

Two things happened at the same time.

One: My cell phone rang. It was my father.

"Robbie, I'm in the neighbourhood. How about I swing by and pick you up?"

Two: Ms Denholm moaned loudly, and Billy's eyes widened in astonishment.

"Your car," he said to Ms Denholm.

"What was that sound?" my father said.

Ms Denholm was standing beside her car. One hand was over her mouth. With her other hand, she reached out gingerly to touch the car's hood. Billy stood helplessly behind her, doing what I was doing: staring at the car. Every single one of the Toyota's windows had been smashed. So had the headlights. There were huge dents in the hood. Ms Denholm moaned again.

"Robbie? What's going on?"

I told my father what had happened.

"Where is the car parked?" he said. "On the street or around the back?"

"Around the back."

A few moments later, I heard my father calling my name.

"Over here, Dad," I called.

He came flying around the side of the house, his coat unbuttoned, his face tense. He looked me over and seemed to breathe easier when he saw that I was unharmed. Ms Denholm didn't even register his presence at first. She was staring at her car as if she couldn't believe what she was seeing. My father looked at it and then at her. He tossed me his car keys. "There's a flashlight in the trunk of my car, Robbie. Get it for me, will you?" He nodded at Billy and then cautiously approached Ms Denholm.

She turned slowly. Her eyes widened when she saw him. She retreated a step, as if she were afraid of him.

"Ms Denholm, my name is Mac Hunter. I'm Robyn's father."

"Her father?" Ms Denholm looked at me for confirmation. I nodded. Her whole body relaxed into a posture of relief. She extended a hand to him.

"Melissa Denholm. Robyn's English teacher."

"So I've heard," my father said. "What happened to your car?"

Ms Denholm looked at the Toyota again and shook her head in disbelief.

"Was anything stolen?" my father said.

Ms Denholm shook her head again.

My father turned to me.

"Robbie," he prompted. "Flashlight."

I trotted around the side of the house to his car, which was parked at the curb out front. When I returned with the flashlight, Ms Denholm was saying, ". . . but she's eighty-two years old and nearly deaf. Besides, she spends her evenings in bed with her TV at almost full volume."

"Are there any other tenants? Anyone who might have seen or heard something?"

"Only Nat," Ms Denholm said. "She's in the rear apartment." She pointed, and my father craned his neck to look up. "But she's not home."

"Was she here when you got home after school?"

Ms Denholm shook her head.

My father turned slowly and surveyed the area. The property was surrounded on three sides by dense cedar shrubs that stood at least two metres high. I could see the second storeys of some of the nearby houses, but I didn't see lights on in any of them.

"Your landlady likes her privacy, I see," my father said. "Still, it's possible someone saw or heard something." He asked Ms Denholm to move away from the car. Then he carefully circled it, staying well back and running the beam of his flashlight over every surface of the car and of the ground around it. It had snowed a few days ago and had stayed cold enough that the snow hadn't melted away, so there was a mishmash of tire tracks and other marks in it. But even I could see that the only distinct footwear impressions around the car were from Ms Denholm's high-heeled boots. She'd made them as she'd circled the car, looking in horror at the damage. When my father finished his inspection, he shook his head. "Can you think of anyone who might have done this?"

Ms Denholm looked at him, the same worried expression on her face that I had seen earlier in the day.

"Are you a police officer?" she said.

"No," my father said. "Why?"

"You sound like one." Something in the way she said it made me think that this was not a good thing, at least as far as she was concerned. I don't know whether or not my father noticed. If he did, he didn't let it bother him.

"But you should call the police," he said, "and report the incident."

Ms Denholm shook her head. "They won't do anything."

My father glanced at me, maybe to see if I knew why she had such a negative view of the police. I just shrugged. "Ms Denholm, your insurance company will want you to file a police report before they pay for any repairs to your car," he said gently. "They'll insist on it. Why don't you let me make the call?"

She looked at him for a few moments, as if trying to decide. Finally, reluctantly, she nodded. My father punched some numbers into his cell phone and reported the incident. When he had finished, he said, "They'll be here as soon as they can. Would you like us to wait with you?"

Ms Denholm shook her head.

"I'll be fine," she said. "Maybe it was one of those homeless people the neighbours are always talking about. There's a shelter for homeless men nearby."

"It's over on Selwyn Street," Billy said. "That's just two blocks from here."

"I've heard people talking. They complain that the homeless take over the park in summer," Ms Denholm said.

My father looked doubtful. "I could understand if your car was broken into and something was stolen, like the stereo. But what reason would a homeless person have to completely trash your car?" he said. "Have there been other incidents of vandalism in the area?" Ms Denholm didn't say anything. She just stared at her battered car.

"I'd feel better if you let us keep you company until the police arrive," my father said. Every time he mentioned the word police, Ms Denholm's face changed ever so slightly. My father was watching her closely. He said, "Has this sort of thing happened before?"

"Thank you for your help," Ms Denholm said. "But

I can take care of things from here. Really, you don't have to worry."

"Ms Denholm — "

"Thank you, Mr. Hunter. Good night, Robyn. Billy."

She went inside.

I glanced at Billy. He looked worried.

We followed my father to his car.

"I'll drive you kids home," he said. "But I want to wait until the police get here."

A cell phone rang. It was Billy's. He answered it and listened for a moment.

"Um . . . I'm with Robyn," he said finally. "No, I didn't forget." He checked his watch. A look of panic crossed his face. "I'm on my way."

"Morgan?" I said when he had finished his call.

"I was supposed to help her with a biology assignment," he said.

"And you forgot."

"Don't tell her, okay, Robyn?"

I promised I wouldn't and shook my head as I watched him scurry for the bus stop. I got into the car with my father.

"You don't think a homeless person wrecked Ms Denholm's car, do you?" I said.

"I've heard people complain about the homeless lingering too long in coffee shops or in the public library or taking over street corners. But I've never heard of a homeless person vandalizing someone's car to that extent for no reason. When someone trashes a car like that, they're usually sending a personal message."

I knew by that familiar expression that something was bothering him.

"What is it, Dad?" I said.

"I'm just thinking."

So was I.

"It didn't take you long to get to Ms Denholm's house after you called me, Dad."

"Like I said, I was in the neighbourhood."

"Did you get my message?"

He nodded.

"Sorry about the change of plans," I said. I explained about the wallet. "I'm glad you were in the neighbourhood. I don't think Ms Denholm would have called the police if you hadn't talked her into it." I told him about the flowers Ms Denholm had received at school.

"When did this happen?"

"Last week."

"Did she call the police?"

"I don't think so." I told my father what she had said.

He asked me a few more questions and then fell into a thoughtful silence.

A police cruiser pulled up opposite Ms Denholm's house and two uniformed police officers got out. My father crossed the street to meet them. They all stood together for a few moments. My father seemed to be doing all the talking. The two police officers went up to the house. My father got back into the car. This time, he put it into gear.

I was half-expecting him to grill me about Ms Denholm on the way home — my father is a naturally inquisitive person; he says it's either an occupational prerequisite or an occupational by-product, he can't decide which. But he surprised me by not asking anything about her.

"So, how's it going with the job you're doing for Ted?" I said, mostly to break the silence.

My father glanced at me. "You know I can't discuss that."

"Ted told Mom and me what you're doing. He told us all about it," I said. "Have you made any progress?"

"Come on, Robbie. You know that any work I do for a client is confidential."

"But it's Ted. He's practically a member of the family."

Up went one of my father's eyebrows. "Oh?" he said. "Has your mother given him an answer?" He meant an answer to Ted's marriage proposal. He tried to sound casual about it, but the searching glance he gave me was anything but casual.

"You know I can't discuss that," I said. "Anything and everything about Mom's personal life is confidential."

My father glanced at me again. Then he reached over and pushed the button that started the CD player. Late sixties rock and roll. Played loud. In what my mother called "Mac's stereo on wheels." Just like a kid.

I sat back and wondered about Ms Denholm's car. Who had smashed it up? And why? And why had

Ms Denholm seemed so reluctant to get the police involved?

It was only after my father had dropped me off that another question occurred to me. How had my father known that he was in Ms Denholm's neighbourhood when he called me? I hadn't mentioned Ms Denholm's address in the message I'd left him. Come to think of it, I hadn't even mentioned it when he had called to ask me if I wanted a lift. He hadn't asked for it, either. In fact, the only thing he had asked was whether Ms Denholm's car was parked out front or in the back, which meant that he already knew where she lived. But *how?*

More to the point, *why?*

Chapter 6

Morgan had been in a bad mood ever since lunchtime, when Billy announced that he was staying after school to meet with Ms Denholm, who had shown up that morning looking ghostly pale except for the dark circles under her eyes.

"What are you meeting about?" Morgan asked.

Billy replied that he had what he modestly called "some pretty good ideas" about set design that he wanted to run by Ms Denholm.

"Ms Rachlis, you mean," Morgan said. "She's the teacher in charge of sets."

Billy's cheeks turned pink. "Ms Rachlis *and* Ms Denholm," he said.

"Okay," Morgan said. "Where and when is the meeting?"

"Why do you want to know that?"

"So I can be there, too. *I'm* working on sets with you, remember?"

Which is when Billy surprised us both by saying

(sweetly, of course) that he appreciated the offer but that he really didn't need Morgan's help at this point and that, as set director, he felt that he would make a more professional impression if he met with Ms Denholm and Ms Rachlis alone instead of dragging his girlfriend along.

Morgan's face morphed into a mask of indignation. She said, "Fine," although it was clear that she regarded the situation as anything but fine. She said, "If that's what you want," her tone conveying that it wasn't at all what *she* wanted. Billy had smiled (still sweetly) and kissed her on the cheek. She (of course) melted — she never failed to melt when Billy kissed her — and that was that. I couldn't figure out whether Billy was totally oblivious to Morgan's feelings or if he had figured out how to do what no one else on the planet was capable of doing: get his own way, despite Morgan's objection, without Morgan vowing revenge in return. Either way, I admired how he handled her.

Well, I *sort of* admired how he handled her, because, although it was true that she wasn't angry with Billy anymore, she was still in a rotten mood. And that mood wasn't likely to improve when I told her what I had to say, which was: "Sorry, but it looks like my plans have just changed. I don't think I can go with you after all."

She glowered at me.

"What do you mean, your plans have changed? You *said* you'd go to the paint store with me. You promised." Not only had Billy finessed her out of the meeting with Ms Denholm and Ms Rachlis, but he had also successfully (astonishingly) talked her into doing an errand for him. Her task: go to the local paint store and come back with an armload of paint samples for Billy's perusal.

"I know I promised," I said. "But something just came up." I nodded toward the street. Morgan followed my gaze.

"Who is that?" she said.

"I think you need glasses," I said. "It's Ted." He was sitting in his car directly across the street. The only reason I could think of for his being there was that he was looking for me.

"I think you need glasses," Morgan said. "Or did Ted suddenly get a whole lot taller, a whole lot younger, a whole lot cuter, and grow a whole lot more hair?"

I shifted my gaze slightly and saw that she wasn't looking where I was looking. Instead, she was staring at a tall, young, and — she was right — incredibly good-looking man with a full head of thick black hair who was standing on the sidewalk on our side of the street.

"If it weren't for the cigarette, he'd be perfect," Morgan said.

"Hmmm," I said absently. I had turned back to Ted's car. Ted was sitting behind the wheel. He seemed to be looking at the school, but he didn't wave at me or give any other sign that he had seen me. What was going on?

"What is he doing?" Morgan said.

Good question, I thought.

"It looks like he's squishing it or something," Morgan said.

"What?" I glanced at Morgan. "What are you talking about?"

"That guy," she said. "He's got an unlit cigarette in his hand and he's squishing it." I looked at him again. Morgan was right. He was rolling a cigarette between his thumb and his first two fingers. "You don't think that's weird? Not to mention that it's littering."

"Maybe he's trying to quit," I said. "Look, I gotta go."

"Go where?"

I pointed to the grey car sitting across the street. Morgan squinted at it.

"What do you think he's doing here? Is he here to see you? Hey, you don't think your mother dumped him again, do you?"

"She never dumped him in the first place," I said. "She just needed a little space."

"Right," Morgan said. "When a guy finally gets his nerve up to propose and the woman he proposes to responds by taking a time-out, she might as well be dumping him."

"They've been back together since before Christmas," I pointed out.

"Then what's he doing here?"

"That's what I'm going to find out."

"I'll wait for you. I really need your help, Robyn." I couldn't have been more surprised if she had suddenly announced that she was going vegan, just like Billy.

"You need *my* help? What for? To carry paint samples?"

"I don't want to just bring back a bunch of paint samples," Morgan said.

"Even though that's what Billy asked you to do?"

"I want to bring back the exact right colours."

"But Billy said — "

"Do you know who else is on the set-design team?" she said, giving a nasty zing to the word *team*. Morgan is not a team player. She detests teamwork. If Morgan ever shines — and she shines all the time — it's as a solo act, which allows her to bask in *all* the glory.

"No. Who?"

"Keisha Minotte."

"So?"

"Keisha has a thing for Billy."

That was news to me. But, "So? Billy has a thing for you."

"She kept him for twenty minutes after our first set-design meeting and asked him all about DARC and how she could join. She says she *loves* birds."

Unfortunately, Morgan didn't feel the same way. She had participated in some DARC activities during the last migration season and had discovered that she abhors birds — especially dead ones — even more than she abhors teamwork.

"I don't think Billy cares how you feel about birds, Morgan."

"Billy doesn't *know* how I feel about birds. Oh, and did I mention that Keisha is a vegan?"

"He loves you, Morgan. And if anyone knows colours, it's you." How could she not? She spends all of her spare time shopping. She's always up on all the latest trends, including the hot new colours. "You'll be fine."

She continued to grumble about Keisha.

"Call me later," I said. I hurried across the street.

Even though I walked directly to Ted's car and stopped right beside it, I had to rap on the window to get his attention. He jolted in his seat, as if my fist had punched right through the glass. The window whirred down.

"Robyn," he said, genuinely startled, which made me think that I had been wrong, that he wasn't waiting for me after all.

"I saw your car. Is everything okay, Ted?"

He nodded, but in a distracted way. He was looking past me at the school. I circled the car, opened the passenger door, and got in. Then I waited.

"Do you know a teacher named Ms Denholm?" he said at last.

"Sure. She's my English teacher."

Ted looked surprised. "I know you've talked about your English teacher. But I don't remember — "

"She's a substitute teacher. She's only been here since Christmas."

Ted nodded and glanced at the school again.

"What's she like?"

"She's nice. Enthusiastic. She's directing the school play. I'm assistant director."

Ted had been gazing at the school all this time,

but now he turned to look at me.

"Your father tells me that her name used to be Bonnie Gold."

Oh.

"Your . . . daughter," I said.

Ted nodded.

That explained why my father had known where Ms Denholm lived. He had done his research. He had probably been checking everything out so that he was one hundred percent sure of his facts before he passed the information on to Ted. If Ms Denholm hadn't already been outside when he'd arrived, he would have found some other way to meet her face to face.

"Your father gave me her new name. He told me where she works and where she lives. He said it was up to me what happened next," Ted said. "He wished me luck."

I could imagine my father doing that. He would have met Ted somewhere, maybe at Ted's condo or maybe in my father's loft. He would have sat directly opposite Ted — when he has something important to say (or to ask), my father always sits directly opposite the person he's talking to so that he can see their reaction — and he would have told Ted what he had found out. He would have laid it out slowly, pausing to allow Ted to digest what was being said. He would have told Ted that he had done all he could and that the rest was up to Ted. And when he wished Ted good luck, he would have been sincere, even though Ted was seeing my mother and had proposed to her, and even though my father still acted like he had a chance of winning my mother back. (I couldn't tell anymore if he really believed it or if it was an act.) He would know that the news he had given Ted was a big deal. He would know that Ted would be nervous about it and that he'd be wondering if his daughter ever thought of him, if she hated him, if she would reject him when he tried to approach her. Because he would know that, my father would be kind. Maybe it was true what my mother said, that he's impossible to live with. But he isn't a bad person.

"I don't know what to do," Ted said. His eyes were uncertain behind the lenses of his glasses. "Can you believe it? I'm terrified. I've been sitting here for nearly an hour and I haven't been able to make myself get out of the car."

"She's really nice, Ted," I said.

"The last time I spoke to her, she told me that she never wanted to see me again."

"That was a long time ago."

He reached inside his coat and pulled out a sheet of paper.

"Mac gave me this," he said, unfolding it and handing it to me. I recognized it immediately. It was a photocopy of Ms Denholm's driver's licence, with her address and her picture on it. My father has a lot of contacts who are willing to do favours for him and a lot of sources who are willing to give a little in return for getting a little.

"It's not a very good picture of her," I said. "She's much prettier in person."

"Her mother was a knockout," Ted said. He quickly added, "Not that your mother isn't."

"She's still in there," I said, nodding at the school. "She's in the auditorium. If you want, I'll show you the way."

Ted turned and looked at the school again. He said nothing for a few moments.

"She's going to be at my school until the end of the year," I said. What I meant was, he didn't have to do anything today if he didn't want to. He could take his time.

He sighed and pulled his keys from the ignition.

"There's no time like the present," he said. He got out of the car. I scrambled out after him. He looked over the roof of the car at me and said, "I'd appreciate it if you would show me the way."

I circled the car, and we crossed the street together. Ted's expression was grim as we approached the school, climbed the steps, and pulled open the big front door. I led him across the atrium and peeked in through the little windows in the auditorium doors. Ms Denholm and Billy were up on the stage. Ms Denholm was closing her thick binder. Billy was standing opposite her, rolling up a big sheet of paper. Ms Rachlis was nowhere to be seen, so I guessed that their meeting had already ended.

"That's her, isn't it?" Ted said, his voice filled with wonder and dread. He swallowed hard.

"Do you want me to introduce you?" I felt sorry for him. He looked terrified.

He stared in through the glass.

"Maybe this isn't the right time," he said. He backed away from the door and then stopped and stood motionless, as if fear had literally paralysed him. He glanced at me and said, "You must think I'm the world's biggest chicken."

"No, I don't," I said.

He drew in another deep breath and pulled himself up straight. "Okay," he said. "Here goes."

He opened the door and plunged into the auditorium. I trailed a few paces behind him, just in case. Just in case of what, though, I wasn't sure.

Once he was inside, Ted hesitated again. He stopped, looked at the stage, took a few steps, and stopped again. I saw his shoulders rise as he drew in another deep breath. He walked slowly down the inclined aisle toward the stage. He was three-quarters of the way there when Ms Denholm squinted out at the rows of seats.

"Who's there?" she said, sounding alarmed. Billy turned around and raised a hand to shield his eyes from the brightness on stage. They were having trouble seeing Ted and me because, although the stage was lit, the rest of the auditorium was dark.

Ted picked up his pace, moving briskly now into the light from the stage. Billy broke into a smile.

"Hi, Ted," he said. "If you're looking for Robyn — "

Ms Denholm relaxed at the sound of my name. "Robyn isn't here," she said.

Ted was standing right in front of the stage now, his head tilted back so that he could look up at Ms Denholm. He said, "Bonnie?"

Ms Denholm stared down at him. Billy looked confused. Ted moved to the left and slowly climbed the five wooden steps that led up to the stage.

"Bonnie," he said again. "Do you remember me?"

I followed Ted up to the stage. I like Ted — a lot. I didn't want him to get hurt. But I felt for Ms Denholm, too. She had been eight years old the last time she had seen her father. According to her driver's licence, she was twenty-four now. The gulf between her and Ted must only have grown in that time.

Ms Denholm was as still as a mannequin. As her eyes searched Ted, Ted's hand went self-consciously to his head. Except for a thick fringe that ran behind his head from ear to ear, Ted's hair was sparse, but I guessed it hadn't been that way the last time Ms Denholm had seen him.

"You're Ted Gold," she said in a quiet voice. "You're my father."

Ted stood rigid on the stage. He seemed to be holding his breath.

"Mom died last year," Ms Denholm said.

"I know." My father must have told him. "I'm sorry."

"When I moved here six months ago," Ms Denholm said, "I knew you lived here. I Googled you. I found out where you work."

"You did?" Ted said. He sounded like someone who had just been handed a ticking, gift-wrapped box and was trying to decide what was inside — a brand new clock or a bomb that was set to detonate.

"I was trying to work up the nerve to call you. I even picked up the phone a couple of times," Ms Denholm said. "But after what I said to you the last time we spoke — "

"That was a long time ago," Ted said. "You were a child."

Ms Denholm looked him over. It was impossible to tell what she was thinking. Then she held up her right hand. Ted stared at it.

"That ring was in my grandmother's family for generations," he said. "Her great-great-grandfather gave it to his only child. Since then, it's been passed to the eldest child. I gave it to your mother for you when you were born."

"I found it in one of her drawers when I was thirteen," she said. "I used to babysit for the man who owned the jewellery store in the town where we lived. Just before I left for university he resized it for me. I've worn it ever since." She smiled nervously at Ted. "I'm glad you're here."

I gestured to Billy to get off the stage so that Ted and Ms Denholm could be alone. It took a few moments before he finally got the picture. He gathered his things and jumped down from the stage. Ms Denholm and Ted didn't notice. They were staring at each other, both wide-eyed and seemingly dazed, as if they couldn't quite believe what they were seeing. I grabbed Billy by the arm and pulled him up the aisle. He kept glancing back over his shoulder.

"What was that all about?" he said as I pushed open the auditorium doors.

"Ms Denholm and Ted haven't seen each other in a long time," I said.

"Oh." He still looked puzzled, and for a moment I thought he was going to ask me all about it. But in the end, all he said was, "Well, she looked happy to see him, and that's good. She seems sad, you know, Robyn?"

"Well, someone *did* trash her car."

"I mean besides that. You heard what she said. Her mom died last year. Maybe it'll make her feel better having Ted around."

I peeked back in through the window in the auditorium door. Ted and Ms Denholm were still on the stage. They were still talking.

"I hope so," I said. I knew Ted was hoping, too.

Billy handed me his backpack to hold while he put on his jacket and dug his cell phone out of his pocket. He made a quick call. When he finished, he said, "Morgan wants me to meet her at the paint store. Want to come?"

I shook my head. Morgan and Billy were my oldest and best friends, but since they'd become romantically involved, they were sometimes hard to be around. I still found it strange to see Morgan, who used to tease Billy all the time for being such a good-guy geek, turn to mush every time Billy beamed at her. And it was weird to see Billy, who up until recently had had more respect for wildlife than he did for people, smiling contentedly at Morgan, who thought animals were just fine so long as they were on plates, on leashes, or confined to zoos.

"I'm going home," I said. "I have a pile of homework to do."

We parted company. Billy veered off toward the school parking lot, and I headed for the bus stop up the street.

The man whom Morgan had pointed out earlier was still standing in front of the school and still worrying an unlit cigarette between the leather-gloved thumb and forefinger of one hand. Tiny shreds of tobacco littered the snow at his feet. He didn't turn when I walked past him, but continued to stare at the school, watching the door as if he were waiting for someone to walk through it. He had been there for at least twenty minutes now in the bitter January cold. I wondered who he was waiting for. He looked too young to be the father of a high-school student, but you never know.

Chapter 7

Friday, January 29

I pushed open the door to my father's loft.

"Robbie!" my father said. "What a pleasant surprise."

What did he mean, surprise? This was my weekend to stay at his place. Had he forgotten? As for the pleasant part, a couple of things told me that he wasn't being one hundred percent truthful about that. The first was the way he looked at Vernon Deloitte, who was sitting opposite him at the kitchen counter. Vern is an ex-police officer like my father. The two of them are business partners. The look my father gave Vern was one of those guarded warning looks that cops give each other when they've been talking business and a civilian suddenly arrives on the scene. The second thing was the way Vern immediately and supposedly casually flipped shut the notebook that had been lying open on the counter in front of him. He greeted me with a great big hello while he discreetly slipped the notebook into his jacket pocket.

"I thought you and Ben were going out tonight," my father said.

"We were."

My father noted my use of the past tense. "Problem?"

"Something came up," I said. Ben had called me right after school and had apologized. He said he had to pick something up downtown. He said it was important. It couldn't wait. "We're getting together tomorrow instead."

My father glanced at Vern before flashing me one of those charming smiles that always irritate my mother. "Does this mean I'll have the pleasure of your company for supper, Robbie?"

"Unless you and Vern are working on something," I said.

"Not at all," my father said. "In fact, Vern was just on his way out."

On cue, Vern stood up. Right. I bet they even thought they were fooling me. I threw my backpack on a chair near the door, pulled off my boots, and hung my coat in the closet. As I was shutting the closet door, I saw Vern hand my father a couple of sheets of notebook paper, which my father slipped into the napkin drawer. I turned away so that they wouldn't know I had seen them. When I glanced at them again, Vern was pulling on the coat that had been draped over the back of his chair. He left. My father and I went down to La Folie, the gourmet restaurant that occupies the main floor of my father's building. In addition to being the restaurant's landlord, my father was good friends with the owner. He ate there regularly. A while after we ordered, I said, "So, Dad, Ted is really happy that you found his daughter. They got together yesterday — at my school."

"I know," my father said.

Of course he did. My father seemed to know everything.

"He told Mom that he thinks you're a modern-day Sherlock Holmes for finding her. And I have to tell you, Dad, I can't think of a better daughter for Ted. Ms Denholm is really nice. Everyone likes her."

"Mmmm," my father said.

Mmmm? That was my father's way of saying, "No comment."

"She is nice, right, Dad? She isn't a crazed axe murderer or anything like that, is she?"

"Not that I'm aware of, Robbie."

"So what's the problem?"

"Who says there's a problem?"

My father is a smart guy, but sometimes not smart enough to realize that I've known him all my life, which means that although I can't read his mind, I usually know when there's something he's not saying.

The waiter appeared and delivered my father's order. My father eyed it appreciatively, rubbed his hands together, and said, "That looks good."

I waited until my meal had been set down in front of me before I said, "Did the police find out who trashed Ms Denholm's car?"

"Not that I'm aware of," my father said.

"You keep saying that, Dad. You sound like a politician who's trying to distance himself from a scandal. What's going on?"

He shook out his linen napkin and laid it on his lap. Before he tucked into his own meal, he looked at my plate and said, "That looks pretty good, too."

In other words, that was the end of any conversation about Ms Denholm.

After we ate, we went back upstairs.

"How about a movie?" my father said.

"Okay."

"I'll make the popcorn."

"Dad, we just ate."

"Robbie, you can't watch a movie without popcorn." Maybe he couldn't, but I could. "It'll only take a few minutes."

There was no point in arguing. When it came to popcorn, I always lost.

"While you're doing that, I'm going to check my messages," I said. "Maybe Ben called."

I fished my cell phone out of my backpack, which was sitting on the chair near the front door where I had left it, and checked the display. There were two messages. The first, according to the readout, was from Ben. I listened to it as I went back into the living room. He had called to tell me where he would meet me the next day. I didn't recognize the second phone number. When I listened to the message, I felt as if the breath had been knocked out of me.

It was Nick.

"Hey, Robyn, you're probably mad at me, which I guess is why I haven't heard from you."

He hadn't heard from *me?* What was he talking about? I had no idea where he was.

"I guess I don't blame you," the message continued. "I just, well, I — "

I couldn't make out most of the rest of his message because there was a roar in the background. It sounded like a gargantuan piece of machinery — maybe an airplane engine. Maybe some kind of interference. Or maybe a crowd of people all shouting at the same time. ". . . coming back . . . love . . . " More noise. What was that? " . . . call . . . "

End of message. I checked the number on the display again and pressed the Call button. All I got was a recorded message: "The number you are calling cannot receive incoming calls."

I listened to Nick's message again, and again I was unable to make out what he had said. After two months with no word at all from him, of not even knowing where he was, Nick had called me, wondering why I hadn't contacted *him.* He had said something about coming back (at least, I think he had) and about loving me (at least, I think that's what he had meant) and had asked me to call (at least, I think so). But call him *where?* I couldn't reach him at the number he'd called from. Had he given a different phone number that had been drowned out by all that noise? Did he realize that I might not have heard it? If he didn't hear from me, would he call again? Or would he assume that I didn't want to speak to him? Knowing Nick —

I don't want to blame my father for what happened next. It wasn't really his fault. I was the one who decided to listen to the message again on my way back to the sofa. I was the one who was so intent on trying to hear what Nick was saying under all that noise that I really wasn't watching where I was going. I didn't see my father sweep out of the kitchen carrying a bowl of popcorn. I guess he didn't see me, either, until it was too late. We collided. I dropped my phone. When I bent to scoop it up, my hand slipped and I must have hit the wrong button because I heard that robot-like voice say, "Message deleted."

No, *no, NO!*

I fumbled with the phone. I punched in my code to retrieve messages. The robot-like voice said, "You have no new messages. You have no saved messages."

I let out a howl.

"Robbie?" My father sounded alarmed. "Robbie, is everything okay?" When I didn't answer — tears rolled down my cheeks as I stared at my cell phone — my father said, "What's wrong?"

"Nick," I said.

My father looked confused. He glanced around as if he expected to see Nick standing in the room with us. Then he zeroed in on my cell phone.

"Nick called you?" he said. I nodded. "Is he okay?" Unlike my mother, who was more relieved than troubled by Nick's disappearance, my father worried about where Nick had gone and why he had left so abruptly. Like me, he was afraid that Nick might have got into trouble again. That was because, unlike my mother and very much like me, my father genuinely liked Nick.

"I don't know," I said. "I couldn't tell. There was a lot of noise in the background. I couldn't make out most of what he was saying. I think he wanted me to call him, but I couldn't hear the phone number." Assuming he had even given one.

"Do you want me to listen and see if I can make it out?"

"I just deleted the message — by mistake."

"Did you call the number on the display?"

I told him about the recorded message.

"That means he was probably calling from a pay phone. Most pay phones in this country don't take incoming calls."

Terrific.

"Was he calling from here in town?"

I shook my head and handed him my phone. He frowned as he checked the incoming calls.

"That's an Alberta area code," he said. "What's he doing out there?"

I wished I knew.

"If you want, I can try to track down the number," my father said. "But if it's a pay phone, I'm not sure how much help that will be."

Tears started to flow again. I was angry — with myself for dropping my phone and deleting Nick's message. With my father, for insisting on popcorn and for not watching where he was going. With Nick for waiting two months and then calling me at the one time I didn't have my phone with me, for picking the worst possible place from which to make his call, for not saying what he had to say clearly enough to be heard over the background noise, and, mostly, for disappearing in the first place. And I was doubly angry, with myself again, for crying like a baby over him. Was I kidding myself? Was I clinging to a false hope? I swiped angrily at the tears on my cheeks. "I think he was telling me that he loves me," I said fiercely, as if it were the worst thing Nick could have said.

"I see," my father said. He looked at me long and hard. "Well, if he was, he'll call back."

If he was.

If he doesn't jump to conclusions, which Nick has a tendency to do.

If he doesn't think that I'm not returning his call because I'm mad at him for disappearing without a word of explanation.

If. If. If.

I couldn't concentrate on the movie. I went back to my room and opened the top drawer of a small chest of drawers where I keep some extra clothes. Nestled in among the T-shirts was a little box that I hadn't touched since New Year's Eve. I picked it up and opened it. Inside were two intertwined gold hearts suspended from a gold chain. On the back was engraved: *To RH. Love you forever. ND.* Nick had sent it to me for Christmas — but I had no idea where he had sent it from or whether he was still there now.

Ben had been with me when I opened the box. When he'd seen what was inside, he'd asked me if he had anything to worry about. I'd told him no. But I hadn't thrown away Nick's gift.

I fingered the intertwined hearts for a moment before dropping them back into the box and slipping it back into the drawer. I wasn't sure what it meant when a guy said he loved you and sent you a token of his supposed love, but didn't tell you where he was or why he had left or if he was ever coming back. But I was pretty sure it wasn't a good sign.

* * *

Later that night, I called the number on the display again — and again. I kept getting the same message.

I couldn't sleep. I lay in bed, thinking about what Nick had said — that he thought he hadn't heard from me because I was mad at him. How could he possibly have heard from me when I didn't know where he was? I stared at my cell phone on the little table beside me, willing it to ring.

It didn't.

Finally I got up and went into the kitchen to get a glass of water. While I was there, I remembered Vern handing some notepaper to my father and my father slipping it into the napkin drawer. I opened the drawer now. There was nothing in it but napkins.

Chapter 8

I was supposed to meet Ben at the drop-in centre for the homeless where we both volunteered and where we had originally met. We were going to spend a few hours there. I would be in the kitchen preparing meals and making sandwiches for the night patrol van that went around the city to make sure that people who slept outside had food and bedding to help them stay warm. Ben would be in the lounge area where he socialized with the homeless people who used the centre and helped them solve any problems they might have. Ben had been volunteering for long enough that he knew what to do if someone needed to see a doctor or a dentist or didn't have bus fare to get to the welfare office. The people who used the drop-in centre regularly seemed to like him. He was kind and respectful and easy to talk to. In fact, those were the qualities that had attracted me to him.

If I didn't hurry up and get going, I would be late. But instead of grabbing my purse and dashing out the door, I found myself lingering in my room, fussing with my hair, and wondering if I should change my sweater. I pulled out the little box that Nick had sent me and stared at it. I told myself that the smart thing to do was to get rid of it and forget about Nick. But neither my heart nor my hands listened to what my brain was saying. I dropped the box into my purse. I wasn't sure what I was going to do with it, but it felt right knowing I had it with me.

An hour later, I was standing on the sidewalk outside the old church that housed the drop-in centre. I drew in a deep breath, climbed the stairs, pushed open the heavy wooden door, and was immediately assaulted by the smell of sweat and coffee, toast and oatmeal, and by the sounds of talking and coughing, sneezing and television. Stamping my feet on the mat in the foyer to get the snow off my boots, I looked around for Ben. He was standing behind a long table on the far side of the hall, dishing out hot cereal to a line of drop-in centre regulars. When he saw me, a smile spread across his face, brightening it the way the morning sun lights the sky. He started toward me. A moment later, while I was hanging up my coat, he slipped an arm around my waist and pulled me close.

"Sorry about cancelling yesterday," he said softly. He kissed me lightly on the cheek.

"That's okay," I said. But I realized that if he hadn't changed his plans at the last minute yesterday, I wouldn't have been downstairs at La Folie when my cell phone rang. I would have been with Ben, and I would have had my phone in my bag with me. I would have heard it ring. I would have answered it. I would have talked to Nick. I would have had the chance to ask him where he was. I would have told him how I felt, which was . . . boy, that was the problem — how *did* I feel? Angry? I had been. Disappointed and hurt, too — how many nights had I cried myself to sleep over Nick's disappearance? But all of those once-sharp feelings had dulled now that he had called me. I would have told him . . .

"I love you," Ben whispered.

"What?" I stared at him, stunned.

Ben pulled back a little. "That's supposed to be a good thing," he said.

"I'm sorry," I said. "You took me by surprise."

He smiled and pulled me close again.

"You're the best thing that's ever happened to me," he said. "You're beautiful and smart and fun to be around. I'm the luckiest guy in the world to have you for a girlfriend. And speaking of surprises — "

Say something, a little voice in my head told me. Tell him how you feel.

"Hey, you two, break it up!" someone called. It was Betty, who was in charge of the kitchen. She was struggling with two large cardboard boxes filled with loaves of bread.

"Do you need help with that?" I said.

"You bet," Betty said. I took one of the boxes from her. "There are two more outside."

I turned to Ben and said, "See you later."

He kissed me on the cheek. I felt relieved as I followed Betty into the kitchen. I knew that I had to say something to Ben. At the very least, I had to tell him that I didn't feel the same way about him as he obviously felt about me. I liked him, but I didn't love him. I thought about how he would react. I imagined the hurt look on his face.

Later, I decided — I would talk to him later. At least, that's what I told myself.

I spent the next few hours in the kitchen, where I washed and chopped vegetables for a soup Betty was making, mixed up a gigantic batch of chili, and peeled a couple of dozen hard-boiled eggs for sandwiches. I had just wrapped the last sandwich when Ben appeared in the kitchen and told Betty that he was springing me.

"I have to run an errand for Mr. Donovan," he said. Art Donovan was the director of the drop-in centre. "Then we're free."

"What kind of errand?"

"The shelter on Selwyn Street is short of blankets. Mr. Donovan asked me to run some over." The drop-in centre was well supplied with just about everything these days, thanks to a generous donation from a very wealthy woman. In fact, come spring, the centre was going to expand. "I've already loaded them into the car. After that, we're going for hot chocolate. I have a surprise for you."

I guessed maybe I had one for him, too. But that would come later, after we had done our errand.

To get to Selwyn Street, we had to drive past the park and the house where Ms Denholm lived. As we got close, I caught sight of something . . . I blinked and looked twice to make sure I was really seeing what I thought I was seeing.

"Stop the car, Ben!"

"Why? What — "

"Just stop the car." It came out sounding like a military order. Ben gave me a strange look, but he pulled over.

"Those two guys look like they're trying to kill each other," he said when he saw what was happening on the sidewalk in front of the house.

It would have been more accurate to say that one of them looked like he was trying to kill the other one. The one who was on the offensive was short, bespectacled, and bald — and all too familiar to me. It was Ted. The man who was under attack, and who looked like he could have nailed Ted with one arm tied behind his back, was younger, taller, and had a full head of thick dark hair. I recognized him, too, even though I had seen him only once before, standing outside my school. Nearby, watching them and looking frantic, was Ms Denholm.

I started to open the car door. Ben grabbed my arm. "Hey, where are you going? You're not going to get involved in that, are you? Because — "

"Call the police, Ben. Call 911."

I jumped out of the car and ran across the street.

Ted was lashing out at the other man, pushing him, hitting him — or trying to — and shouting at him, "Stay away from her. You stay away from her!" The other man appeared to be defending himself.

Ms Denholm tried several times to grab Ted's arm and pull him away, but without success. She looked at me with wild eyes.

"Make them stop," she said, as if I could possibly have any control over a situation like this. "Make them stop."

I knew — because my father had told me — that it was stupid *in the extreme* to try to break up a fight unless you were one hundred percent positive that you knew what you were doing. "And by that, Robbie," he had said, "I mean, unless you've had some training, which — trust me — most people haven't. If you see a fight, even if you think someone is going to be seriously hurt, don't wade in and try to stop it. Call the police. Let them handle it."

I glanced around. Ben was getting out of the car now, his cell phone in his hand. He shouted something to me, but I didn't hear because his voice was drowned out by the sound of sirens. A squad car squealed up to the curb and two uniformed police officers got out. A second car pulled up right after the first. One more uniformed police officer got out. Another one stayed in the car, talking on the radio. The three police officers approached the scene. One of them announced police presence officially. Another one looked directly at me and asked, "Is anybody armed?"

I hadn't seen any weapons. I couldn't imagine that Ted had one, but I wasn't sure about the other man. Besides, I had just arrived. I turned to Ms Denholm for an answer. She shook her head. The police officers looked at each other. One of them took Ted by the arm and another grabbed the other man. They cautioned both of them, escorted them to separate squad cars, and put them inside. The third police officer turned to Ms Denholm and me. He said, "Can you tell me what happened?"

"I didn't see how it started," I said. "I was just passing by."

"That man has been threatening me," Ms Denholm said.

"Which man?" the police officer said.

"The younger man. His name is Mikhail Mornov. He's my ex-boyfriend."

"And the other man?" the police officer said.

"He was trying to get Mikhail to leave me alone."

By now a small crowd had gathered. I wondered where the people had come from. The closest houses were at least ten metres away on either side. There were no houses opposite, just the large park. But police cars have an almost magical quality — they draw spectators the way an ice cream truck draws children. One of these people, or maybe a neighbour, must have phoned the police, because there was no way the police could have responded so quickly to Ben's call.

I saw a woman carrying two supermarket bags filled with groceries push partway through the crowd. She was wearing a heavy winter coat and had her hood pulled up against the wind, but I was pretty sure it was Ms Rachlis, the art teacher at school. She stopped at the fringes of the crowd and said something to one of the bystanders. Then I heard thumping, and I turned toward the two police cruisers behind me. Ms Denholm's ex-boyfriend was pounding on the window from the inside. One of the police officers went to the car and ducked down in front of the window. He must have said something, because the thumping stopped. The police officer who was talking to Ms Denholm said, "I'm going to ask you to come down to the police station, Miss."

Ms Denholm looked in alarm at the police cruiser in which her ex-boyfriend was confined.

"Don't worry," the police officer said. "You don't have to talk to him. You don't even have to see him. I promise. I'll call another car to drive you to the police station."

"We can take you," I said to Ms Denholm. I glanced at Ben. "Can't we, Ben?"

"Of course," Ben said. The police officer told us which police station they were going to, and Ben opened the door for Ms Denholm.

We drove in silence. Ms Denholm didn't say anything and I didn't think it was my place to ask questions. When we got to the police station, Ben got out and opened the door for her. After he slipped back behind the wheel, he said, "What was that all about?"

I held up a hand. I had my cell phone out and had just dialled my father's phone number. It was an automatic reflex — the police were involved, my father used to be a police officer, my father knew a lot of other police officers; therefore, my father would know what do to. Only after I had told him what had happened and he'd said, "I'll be there as soon as I can," did I realize that my first call should have been to my mother. I punched in her phone number.

"Ted?" she said. "In a *fight*? Are you sure?"

I couldn't blame her for doubting me. If ever there was a person you'd think would never get into a street fight, it was Ted.

"I'm sure," I told her. "He's at the police station."

"They *arrested* him?"

"I don't know, but they put him in a police car and took him to a police station." I told her which one. I decided to wait until she arrived before I confessed that I had called my father.

"Now what?" Ben said.

"I guess we should wait."

"Do you want to go inside?"

I looked at the police station and shook my head.

"They don't like you hanging around unless you have business there," I said.

"You know one of those guys?"

"My mother is going out with him. He's a really nice person. I've never seen him act like that before."

"He must have had a good reason," Ben said.

According to Ms Denholm, he had been trying to protect her. I told Ben about Ted and Ms Denholm. I also told him about the flowers and about what had happened to Ms Denholm's car, and how Ms Denholm was obviously afraid of something — or, it now appeared, of *someone*. I said that it probably didn't help that her landlady was practically deaf and wouldn't be able to hear if anything happened.

Someone rapped on the passenger-side window. I jumped, my heart pounding.

"Geez, Dad," I said, pushing the button to lower the window and shivering in the January chill, "you startled me."

"Is Ted still inside?" he said.

"I haven't seen him come out."

"I'll go and see what's happening. You two should take off. Depending on whether they've charged him or not, this could take some time."

After my father disappeared inside the police station, Ben turned the key in the ignition. "We should deliver these blankets. Then we can go and get some hot chocolate," he said.

"I'd like to wait a little longer, Ben, if it's okay with you."

He didn't argue with me.

My mother arrived a few minutes later. She hurried toward the police station, one hand holding her unbuttoned coat closed, her head down against the chilly wind. I got out of the car.

"Mom!"

Her head bobbed up. "Robyn. Is Ted still here?"

I nodded.

"I'm going to go and sort this out. You should go home."

"But, Mom — "

"There's nothing you can do here, Robyn. And it's too cold to sit around out here waiting. I'll call you later. I'm sure everything will be fine."

"But — " I'd been going to tell her that my father

was inside, but it was too late. She was already rushing through the main door.

I got back into the car and we waited. And waited. The temperature inside the car plummeted. Our breath hung in front of us in little clouds. But Ben didn't complain. He didn't pester me with questions, either. He was nice about it. He always was. So why wasn't I as crazy about him as Morgan thought I should be?

Finally Ted emerged with Ms Denholm. He looked pale and shaky and had a bandage over one eye and what looked like a cut on his lip. One side of his face was swollen. A moment later, my mother appeared and hurried to catch up with them. I couldn't hear what they were saying, but Ted was shaking his head, which didn't seem to make my mother happy. Finally she threw up her arms. Ted moved close to her and said something else, which seemed to calm her down. She nodded and Ted kissed her on the cheek — at the exact moment that my father came out of the police station. He stopped and stared at Ted and my mother like an overprotective father who had just caught his teenaged daughter in the arms of the neighbourhood bad boy. It occurred to me then that although my father had known about Ted for several months and had even seen Ted at my mother's house, he had never witnessed my mother and Ted being affectionate with each other. He seemed to be having trouble processing what he was seeing.

My mother noticed my father before Ted did. I'm

pretty sure she registered the stunned expression on his face because, almost defiantly, she pressed closer to Ted. That's when Ted turned and saw my father. He stepped smartly away from my mother — which was not at all what the neighbourhood bad boy would have done. My mother grabbed his arm and pulled him close again. By then, my father's expression had changed. He looked like his normal, casual self — or maybe he was just doing his best to give that impression. Ted said something else to my mother and then raised a hand to flag down a passing taxi. He helped Ms Denholm into it and climbed in after her. My mother watched them go. She turned to my father. She did not look happy. They spoke for a few minutes before they parted, my father heading for his car, my mother for hers.

"I have to go, Ben," I said, reaching for the door handle.

"What about my surprise?"

"I'm sorry. But my mother's upset."

He looked disappointed, but he didn't argue with me. "Go ahead," he said. "And I'd better drop off those blankets. They must be wondering where they are. I'll call you later, okay?"

I caught up with my mother just as she was getting into her car, and slid into the passenger seat beside her.

"What happened?" I said.

My mother's face was sombre. "They charged Ted with assault," she said. "There were two witnesses — a man who was in the park across the street walking his dog, and a woman who was on her way to the store. They both said the same thing. They both said that Ted ran out of the house where his daughter lives, went directly to a man who was standing outside on the sidewalk, and started shoving him aggressively."

"Aggressively? Ted?"

"I know," my mother said. "It doesn't sound like him, does it? He claims the man was threatening his daughter. The trouble is that, according to the witnesses, Ted didn't even speak to the man before he started shoving him. And when the man refused to go away, Ted hit him. The witnesses said that the man had no choice but to defend himself. One of them called the police."

"What did Ms Denholm say?"

"She told the police that the man — her ex-boyfriend — has been harassing her. She said she's pretty sure that he trashed her car earlier this week." She looked at me. "She said that you and your father were there when she reported the incident. Why didn't you tell me?"

My mother had been at her office working when I got home that night, and she'd been gone the next morning by the time I woke up.

"At the time, I didn't know she was Ted's daughter," I said. "She was just my substitute English teacher. How is Ted, Mom? It looks like he was hurt."

"He's gone to the hospital to get himself checked over, but I think he's okay. He's just shaken up — and worried about his daughter." She sighed. "Poor Ted.

After all these years, he finally finds her, but instead of a happy reunion, he's got a whole new set of problems to contend with."

* * *

Ted showed up at the house a couple of hours later. He had a fresh bandage on the cut above his eye and a butterfly suture on his lip, which had become swollen since the last time I'd seen him. His cheek had turned reddish-blue and was still swollen. My mother threw her arms around him and hugged him tightly.

"Come in," she said.

Ted shook his head. "I'm on my way over to Bon— to Melissa's. It's going to take me a while to get used to calling her that. All these years, I've been thinking of her as Bonnie. She's scared, Patricia. She says her ex-boyfriend has been stalking her."

"*Stalking* her?" My mother's eyes widened. "Has she reported him to the police? What are they doing about it?"

"She reported him to the police in Edmonton — that's where she was living before she moved here. She says they didn't take her seriously. She says that the reason she moved here was to get away from him. But he tracked her down. He trashed her car — which, apparently, he denies. She reported it to the police and they say they investigated, but . . . " He shook his head in disgust. "As far as I can tell, the police here aren't taking her seriously, either. He showed up at her house this afternoon while I was there. I was just making it clear that he was to stay away from her, that's all. After all this time — " His voice broke off. "Patricia, I don't want anything to happen to her. You understand that, don't you?"

"Of course I do."

He kissed my mother on the cheek. "Thank you," he said. "I have to go. I'll call you."

Fifteen minutes after he left, the doorbell rang again. This time I answered.

"Dad, what are you doing here?" I glanced around nervously. If my mother saw him, she would be furious. The rule was that my father wasn't supposed to show up at my mother's house unless she invited him, which she never did.

"Robyn?" my mother called. "Did I hear the doorbell again? Did Ted come back?" I heard the rustling of her robe. Then: "What brings you here, Mac?" The ice in her tone was a sharp contrast to the warmth with which she had greeted Ted.

"I wanted to talk to you about what happened," my father said. "Has Ted told you everything?"

"He was just here, Dad."

My mother shot me a furious look that was intended to convey an emphatic message: her business was none of my father's business.

"You haven't answered my question, Mac," she said.

"What did Ted tell you?"

"Excuse me?" my mother said. What she really meant was, How dare you stick your nose into my personal business?

"Patti — "

My mother winced when he called her that. She hated that name. She insisted on being called Patricia. My father resisted.

"Good night, Mac." She started to turn away.

"There's something I think you should know about Ted's ex-wife and his daughter," my father said.

My mother spun around. "Look, Mac, I appreciate what you did for Ted. But I wish you had recommended someone else to find his daughter for him because, frankly, I don't want you involved in anything that has to do with me and Ted."

"Do you really think I *wanted* to be involved?" my father said. "I gave Ted several names. Any one of them could have done what I did. But he insisted that I take the job. He said he wanted someone he could trust."

My mother stared at him. "Why on earth would he trust you?"

"Mom!"

My mother turned to me. "Go to your room, Robyn."

I started to go, but then my father spoke again, refocusing my mother's attention.

"Patti — "

"It's Patricia," my mother said. "How many times do I have to tell you? My name is Patricia."

I decided to stay where I was. After all, I knew Ms Denholm better than either of them did.

"Patricia," my father said, for the first time ever that I had heard. He did not look happy. "Melissa Denholm, formerly known as Bonnie Gold, then

Bonnie Duguid, claims that she is being stalked by her ex-boyfriend. However, neither the police nor I could find any evidence of this. In fact — "

"Neither the police nor *you?* What does this have to do with you?" My mother crossed her arms over her chest.

"Ted hired me to find his daughter, and I did. I believe in being thorough. It's been sixteen years since Ted last saw her. I thought he would appreciate knowing something about her. I had Vern do a background check on her."

My mother eyed him suspiciously.

"A few of the people Vern was chasing down returned his calls after Ted had already reunited with his daughter."

I remembered seeing Vern at my father's place with his notebook open. I remembered him handing some notebook pages to my father and my father slipping them into the napkin drawer.

"And?" my mother said in a still-icy tone.

"*And* in the matter of Melissa Denholm and her ex-boyfriend Mikhail Mornov, the only charges that were ever laid were charges against Melissa Denholm."

"*What?*"

"For assaulting Mikhail Mornov — that charge was laid by the police and subsequently withdrawn at the insistence of Mornov. And for vandalizing Mikhail Mornov's car — that charge was laid by Mornov's father and was subsequently withdrawn, again at the insistence of Mornov."

My mother stared at my father in silence for a few moments. Then she said, "What are you saying, Mac?"

"Ted doesn't know much about his daughter. He saw her a couple of times when she was a little girl. I tried to explain to him about her history and how that may have affected her. I thought you should know, Patti. Maybe you can help him."

"What do you mean, her history?" my mother said.

"Melissa's mother was terrorized by a stalker," my father said. My mother's expression changed from hostile to worried.

"Terrorized?"

"After Beth Gold left Ted, she remarried — to a James Duguid. Apparently it was a pretty rocky marriage. It turned really nasty when Beth finally left him. He didn't take it well. He began to stalk her. He used every trick in the book. He killed the family pet — Melissa's cat — "

My mother gasped.

"—slashed the tires on Beth's car, broke into her house, made threatening phone calls."

"Please tell me she went to the police," my mother said.

"She did. And they followed up. But Duguid was smart. They never got anything on him. And he tried to make it sound as if she was mentally unstable. Like I said, it was nasty. Then Duguid applied for joint custody — he'd legally adopted Melissa after he and Beth married. Beth must have been worried that he might actually get it. She fled with Melissa. From what Vern and I were able to find out, she moved a couple of times, but James always found her. She and Melissa went underground."

"Underground?" My mother shook her head. "What do you mean?"

"They vanished. Beth changed their names — informally, not formally. She didn't want to leave a paper trail. Somehow she managed to get a new birth certificate issued to Melissa — probably illegally. They moved to a small town. She didn't get a phone. She gave up all her credit cards. She didn't get a driver's licence. She worked at menial jobs and always insisted on being paid in cash. She didn't have a bank account."

"In other words," my mother said, "she made sure that neither her name nor her daughter's would show up in any files or databases anywhere."

No wonder Ted hadn't been able to track her down.

"She kept a close eye on Melissa. She was home-schooled her in her elementary years and did high school through correspondence."

"The poor thing must have had a lonely child-hood," my mother said.

My father nodded. "People thought Beth was eccentric. But really she was terrified that James Duguid would find her, and she was convinced that if he did, he would kill both her and Melissa. She spent most of her life hiding. She cut herself off from the world to try to protect her daughter. She didn't surface until about eighteen months ago — right after

James Duguid was killed in a bar fight."

"I heard Ms Denholm tell Ted that her mother died a year ago," I said.

That's when my mother noticed I was still there. She gave me a sharp look but didn't order me to my room again.

"By the time James Duguid was out of her life, Beth was in the late stages of breast cancer," my father said. "And Melissa . . . " He looked directly at my mother. "Melissa had a pretty tough upbringing. Every time she left the house — and from what Vern found out, it wasn't very often — her mother held her breath until she came back again. If Melissa was even five minutes late returning home, she'd find her mother in tears."

"Poor thing," my mother said. I couldn't decide whether she was referring to Ms Denholm or her mother.

"When Melissa started going out with boys, she and her mother had a big blow-up. Their first, according to Vern's sources," my father said. "Melissa's mother drilled it into her head that men who take too much of an interest can be dangerous. You know how it is with men who turn out to be stalkers. They start off flattering a woman with excessive attention. Then they become overly possessive — they never want to let the woman out of their sight. They want to control her. They gradually isolate her from her family and friends. Then they become abusive. If the woman defies them or, heaven help her, tries to leave them, they get violent. According to a woman who knew

Beth just before she died, Melissa had witnessed all of this between her mother and James Duguid. She wanted her life to be different from her mother's. She wanted to meet someone nice and get married and have a family. But it turned out that, despite what she wanted, she had learned from her mother that it was dangerous to get too close to a man you don't know well or to let him get too close to you."

"It's hard to get to know someone, let alone trust him, if you're not willing to let him get close," my mother said.

My father looked at my mother for a moment. I wondered what he was thinking. Was he remembering her kissing Ted?

"Beth and Melissa had an even bigger fight when Melissa decided that she wanted to go to university," he said. "Beth wanted her to stay home and remain hidden so that James couldn't track her down. Melissa refused. She enrolled in university against her mother's wishes. She dated while she was there, but never for long. Whenever a guy showed more than casual interest in her, she backed off."

"Was Mikhail Mornov one of those men?"

My father nodded. "He was in love with her," he said. "At least, that's what people told Vern. But his attention made Melissa nervous. The closer he tried to get, the more she backed off until finally she ended the relationship. When Mornov tried to win her back again, she accused him of stalking her. She kept calling the police about him, but they never found any evidence of wrongdoing on his part. In fact, according to police records, she was the one who behaved aggressively toward him."

"Are you sure, Mac?"

"You know Vern," my father said. "You know how he works. I wouldn't be telling you if I wasn't sure."

My mother didn't argue with him. However she felt about him personally, I think she knew he would never treat something this important lightly.

"And Ted knows this?"

"I told him." He sighed. "There's no question that his ex-wife was being stalked. I'm sure Melissa filled him in on the details of her life with her mother. But I don't think he's willing to consider that Melissa may have developed serious psychological problems as a result, at least insofar as men are concerned."

"That's an opinion, Mac," my mother said. "From an ex-police officer, not from a qualified mental health professional."

"Granted," my father conceded. "Look, Patti — *Patricia* — I have no intention of interfering in your personal affairs. But I thought, in light of your . . . relationship with Ted, that you should be aware of the situation."

My mother waited.

"Mornov told the police that he just wanted to talk to Melissa," my father said.

I wasn't one hundred percent sure, but it sounded as if he believed this.

"Well, of course he told them that," my mother said. "If he were stalking her, surely you wouldn't expect him to tell them the truth."

"He trashed her car, Dad. Billy and I both saw it. So did you."

"We saw the damaged car," my father said.

My mother eyed him closely. "But?"

"Mornov has an alibi."

"Alibi?" my mother said. "What kind of alibi?"

"According to what Robbie told me, Melissa's car must have been damaged sometime between the time she and Billy saw it when they arrived at her house and the time they went outside again so that Melissa could drive them home — in other words, between about seven-fifteen and eight-thirty. Does that sound right to you, Robbie?"

I nodded.

"Mornov has an alibi for that time period. He's been staying with his uncle, a tile importer, since he arrived in town two weeks ago. He was helping out at the warehouse from four in the afternoon that day until just before midnight."

"According to his *uncle*," my mother said with a snort. "I suppose the police accepted that explanation."

"They checked with some of the warehouse employees."

"Who just happen to depend on Mornov's uncle for their livelihood," my mother said. "Come on, Mac. You're not going to tell me that you think they're credible, are you? They could have told the police that he was there because Mornov's uncle made it clear that they would lose their jobs if they didn't."

Instead of answering my mother directly, my

father turned to me. "Was Melissa in her apartment the whole time you and Billy were there with her?"

I started to say yes, but then I remembered. "She went downstairs to speak to her landlady."

"Do you remember how long she was gone?"

"Fifteen minutes," I said. I had looked at my watch. I explained about Ms Denholm's landlady. My father made a note of her name.

"I'll talk to her," he said.

"Talk to her about what?" my mother said.

"Maybe she saw something or heard something."

"She's pretty deaf, Dad," I said.

"Surely the police talked to her already," my mother said. Then her face darkened. "What are you suggesting, anyway?"

"I'm not sure that I'm suggesting anything. But there were witnesses to what happened today."

My mother knew that. She was the one who had told me.

"They all said the same thing," my father said. "They said Ted attacked Mornov and threatened him."

A troubled look appeared in my mother's eyes.

"This girl has had a rough ride, Patt— Patricia. And the young man, Mornov — by all accounts he's a decent guy. He's never been in any kind of trouble that Vern could find out about."

"And Vern has done as thorough a check on Mornov as he has on Melissa, I suppose," my mother said.

"Well, maybe not as thorough," my father admitted. "We were looking into Melissa Denholm, not Mikhail Mornov."

My mother shook her head.

"He can't be all that decent," she said at last, "if he's bothering Melissa when she's made it clear she wants nothing to do with him. She moved here to get away from him. So what is he doing here? Why did he show up at her house when she's made it perfectly clear that he is not welcome in her life?"

"I don't know yet."

"*Yet?*"

"What about the flowers?" I said. "You said Mornov arrived in town two weeks ago. The flowers arrived right after that."

My mother turned to me. "What flowers?"

I filled her in.

"Well, what about them?" she said to my father.

"I checked out the florist that Robyn said they came from. Garden of Eden, right?"

I nodded. "And?"

"Well, there's no such place in town or anywhere around here that I could find," my father said. "And the flowers were left in the school office at a time when it just happened that no one was there. So whoever sent them obviously took pains to make sure they couldn't be traced."

"Anyone like, say, a stalker?" my mother said.

"It's possible."

"*Possible?*" My mother threw up her arms.

"Look. Something doesn't add up. Call it a feeling. Call it a hunch. But from everything that Vern has found out, it's clear that Melissa has a history of unpredictable behaviour. I thought Ted should be aware of that. There's no question that she's afraid of this man. But given what Vern has been able to find out and what's happened in the past two weeks, it's possible that her fear is irrational, based on her mother's experience. And it's possible that she thinks that by accusing Mornov of stalking her, she can make him go away."

My mother kept shaking her head.

"Patti — Patricia, the two of them were going out. Then, according to what he told the police, she suddenly dropped him. He says he has no idea why. When he tried to talk to her to find out what the problem was, she started accusing him of harassing her. But the only accusations that were ever proven or substantiated, and the only charges that were ever laid, have to do with *her* harassing *him*."

"If you ask me," my mother said, "the whole problem would be solved if he simply took the hint and left her alone."

Maybe my father was right. Maybe Ms Denholm had been affected by her mother's experience. It was hard to imagine that she hadn't been. But that didn't mean she was wrong about Mikhail Mornov.

"I saw her when she got those flowers, Dad," I said. "She really looked scared."

My father nodded, but he didn't seem convinced.

"Have you told Ted everything you've just told me?" my mother asked.

My father nodded.

"What did he say?"

"He said he didn't want me meddling in his daughter's life."

"Maybe you should listen to him, Mac."

"But there's something about this that isn't right."

"Maybe," my mother said. "But Ted is a sensible man. Maybe we should just let him get to know his daughter in his own way, in his own time. If you're right, if she has problems, Ted will figure it out. And if his daughter needs help, Ted will make sure she gets it."

My father looked doubtful. But he finally nodded.

* * *

If he had been anyone else but my father, I wouldn't have given a single moment's thought to what he had said. But he was my father. And something was clearly bothering him. That night, after he'd left, I thought back to everything I had personally seen and heard.

Like the flowers. Ms Denholm barely knew me when I brought them to her classroom. But she had made me open them right there in front of her rather than opening them herself. I tried to think whether any other teacher would have asked me to do something like that. And if she was as scared as she looked, why hadn't she called the police? On the other hand, she had shown them to Ms Rachlis, so that made two people who had seen — and could tell other people about — how upset she had been.

Then there was the car. My father was right — I had seen the car when Billy and I arrived at Ms

Denholm's house, and there had been nothing wrong with it then. But there had been a lot wrong with it an hour and a quarter later when Ms Denholm insisted on driving us home. And the look on her face . . . If she hadn't been truly frightened, she had put on a good act.

I remembered the performance she had given in the auditorium, when she had transformed herself from a sweet English teacher into a convincing gang leader. She had a flair for drama, that was for sure.

Was there something to what my father had said? Did Ms Denholm have problems? Had she been damaged by a lifetime of witnessing her mother's terror? And what about the information that Vern had unearthed? There was a police record on Ms Denholm, but none on Mikhail Mornov. Did that mean that he was a cunning stalker who knew how to avoid detection? Or were my father's doubts about what had happened well-founded? Was an unbalanced Ms Denholm trying to rid herself of Mikhail Mornov by accusing him of stalking her? If that was the case, I felt sorry for Ted.

* * *

Later that evening, I took the small box out of my purse. I opened it and looked at the intertwined hearts. Where are you, Nick? You called me once. Why don't you call me again? I dug out the phone book and looked up Nick's aunt's phone number. She sounded surprised to hear from me. She sounded more surprised by my question.

"I haven't heard from him in a over a month," she

said. "Actually, for longer than that. I assumed he was still angry at me because of Glen." Glen was her boyfriend. He and Nick didn't like each other, which was why Nick hadn't moved in with his aunt as he had originally planned. "What happened, Robyn? Did you and Nick break up?"

I looked down at the hearts.

"Something like that, I guess," I said.

"Well, if I hear from him, I'll let you know."

"Ask him to call me," I said.

She said she would. I put down my cell phone and picked up the hearts. I stared at them for a few moments. Then I fastened the chain around my neck.

Chapter 9

SUNDAY, JANUARY 31

I should have spent Saturday night at my father's place — it was my weekend to be with him. But my mother had been worried about Ted and, because of that, I was worried about her. So I stayed at her place instead. But I felt bad for my father, too. He had only been trying to do what he thought was the right thing. So I went over to his place the next morning. He had just finished packing a suitcase when I got there.

"Robbie," he said. "I was just going to call you."

"Are you going somewhere, Dad?"

"Zurich."

"Zurich?" He hadn't said a word about a trip to Zurich. "Since when? And — " Uh-oh. " — what's that smell?"

"What smell?"

"You're wearing aftershave."

"I always wear aftershave, Robbie."

"Yeah, but isn't that the stuff — " I sneezed. " — Mom

gave you the Christmas before you two separated?"

My father looked vaguely embarrassed.

"It seemed a shame to waste it," he said. If you ask me, seeing my mother with Ted had triggered old memories. That was fine with me. But, "Dad, I'm allergic to it, remember?" I sneezed again, twice.

His face flushed, a rarity for my father.

"I'll wash it off," he said when I sneezed for a third time. He handed me a tissue.

"Too late," I said. "I'll be sneezing for an hour now."

But he washed it off anyway and even changed his shirt.

"Sorry, Robbie," he said. "I forgot."

"How come you're going to Zurich all of a sudden?" I said. "Is it Hal-related?"

Hal was an old friend of my father's from high school. He was also the manager of an old but still famous and successful rock band whose members all had houses in Switzerland and the Caribbean and, I think, Manhattan.

"Sort of. And it's not really all that sudden. Mitch is getting married." Mitch was the drummer. "Again," he added. "To an actress." He mentioned the bride-to-be's name. She was the hottest thing on TV. "I was invited. He even arranged for a plane ticket. And Hal invited me to come over ahead of time, make a vacation out of it. At first I didn't think I'd be able to get away, but, what with everything that's been happening, maybe it's a good idea for me to get out of town for a while." He meant until Ted sorted things out with his daughter — and with my mother. He was right. It probably was a good idea. "So I called Hal last night and said I was on my way."

"That's great, Dad." I sneezed again. This time he passed me a handful of tissues.

"*Gesundheit,*" he said.

"How long will you be gone?"

He shrugged. "Two weeks." He didn't say so, but I think he was hoping that everything would have calmed down by then.

The buzzer sounded.

My father glanced at his watch before pushing the intercom button.

"It's me," a voice said. "It's Ted."

My father glanced at me. He pushed another button to release the downstairs door. I heard Ted's footsteps, first on the way up to the second floor, then climbing quickly and steadily to the third floor where we were. My father moved to the door to open it.

"Ted," he said. "Good to see you. I'm afraid I'm in a bit of a rush — "

Ted pushed his way into the foyer, his face red, his glasses fogged up now that he was inside where it was warm.

"I asked you for your help and what do you do?" he said, standing so close to my father that he had to tilt his head back to look him in the eyes. "You launch an investigation into my daughter, without any authorization from me. You question her landlady."

My father had said he was going to talk to Ms

Denholm's landlady. He must have done it last night, despite agreeing with my mother to leave the matter alone. My father doesn't like loose ends.

"I thought it would be wise to have all the facts," he said.

"What you mean is, you don't believe my daughter," Ted countered. "Patricia said that you think she damaged her own car."

My father remained remarkably calm.

"I'm just trying to get things straight in my own mind," he said. "The fact is, Ted, Melissa was out of her apartment for fifteen minutes the night her car was vandalized. But her landlady said that she was downstairs for just a minute to help her open a jar of — "

Ted cut him off. "The woman is old and deaf and forgetful," he said. He was practically shouting. "You're spreading rumours about my daughter and making unsubstantiated accusations. Thanks to you, the police aren't taking her seriously."

"Ted, it was never my intention — "

Ted cut him off again. "To make matters worse," he said, spluttering, "you went behind my back and reported this all to Patricia. I should have listened to her from the start. She always wanted to keep a distance from you. Now I see why. You just can't stand that she's happy with me, can you?"

My father waited until Ted ran out of steam. He spoke quietly when he said, "I don't make accusations, Ted. That's not my style. But I am concerned. There's something about this that just isn't right."

"I came to tell you this face to face, Mac, so there'd

be no misunderstanding. Keep your nose out of my business from now on. I don't want your help and I don't need your concern. Do you understand? I can take care of this myself."

My father glanced at his watch again. I could tell he wanted to argue with Ted. My father doesn't like to be told he's wrong when he believes that he's right, even if nobody else thinks so. He also hates to walk away from what he considers to be a misunderstanding without first clearing things up. But, to my surprise, all he said was, "I understand how you feel. Now if you'll excuse me, I have a plane to catch."

Ted stood his ground for a few seconds, blocking my father's way. He'd been all wound up for a fight. Now that there wasn't going to be one, he seemed almost disappointed.

"Lock up for me, will you, Robbie?" my father said.

Ted spun around like he was on fire.

"Robyn." His face turned crimson. "I didn't see you."

I had guessed as much. He wouldn't have spoken to my father the way he had if he'd known I was listening. His shoulders slumped. My father picked up his suitcase and kissed me on the cheek. Ted moved aside to let him pass.

Ted watched him go before he turned back to me. "I guess if I offered to drive you home, you'd say no, huh?" he said.

I didn't particularly want to go home. But if I declined Ted's offer, he would think I was mad at him, and I wasn't. I was sorry he was angry with my father. I also sympathized with how he must feel. It was like my mother had said. Finding his daughter was supposed to have made Ted happy, but instead it had created a whole new set of problems.

"You could drop me at Morgan's," I said.

Ted attempted a smile. He looked worried and exhausted.

I locked my father's door and we went downstairs. Ted had just opened the car door for me when his cell phone rang.

"Excuse me for a minute, Robyn," he said. He stepped away a few paces so that he could have his conversation privately — well, as privately as is possible on a downtown street. I got into the car.

My nose started to tickle again. I dug in my bag for some tissues. I didn't have any. I dipped into my coat pockets. There were no tissues in there, either. The tickling got worse. I reached for Ted's glove compartment. Ted is one of those people who don't take any chances. He always travels with road maps, a first-aid kit, an emergency roadside kit (flares and reflector signs that he can put behind the car to alert oncoming drivers if, for any reason, he has to stop in the middle of the road), and a supply of tissues. I popped the compartment, expecting to find a pristine box. And I did.

It was sitting right next to the gun.

* * *

My father used to carry a gun. He had to. He was a police officer. My mother never liked it. She never got used to the fact that he was armed. She believes (probably rightly) that people who are armed are likely to have to use their weapon and that people who have to use weapons are far more likely than the average person to have a weapon used on them. When my father came home from work, he was supposed to lock his gun in a special box, and I was "never ever, do you hear me, Robyn, I'm not kidding," (that was my mother speaking) to even think about touching it.

So to say I was surprised to see a gun sitting in Ted's glove compartment would be an understatement.

At first, I was stunned.

Then I was baffled.

I thought, It must be a fake.

It had to be. Ted wasn't the kind of man who would own a gun. He certainly wasn't the kind of man who, even if he did own one, would keep it in the glove compartment of his car. It wasn't legal to transport a gun that way, even if you had a permit to carry one, and I couldn't for the life of me think why Ted would have applied for such a permit, much less been given one.

So it *had* to be a fake. Didn't it?

I would like to say that I obeyed my mother. I can say that I never got curious enough — or stupid enough — to attempt to handle my father's gun on my own. But he let me hold it a couple of times, with no ammunition in it, just to feel it. And he let me shoot it — just once, on a firing range, after taking all the proper precautions. I discovered two things. One:

the gun was much heavier than I had expected. And two: when I squeezed the trigger the way my father had shown me and the gun went off, my whole body jumped with the force of it and, just like that, I knew that shooting and getting shot wasn't anything like they showed it on most TV programs or in most movies. Getting shot wasn't like getting stung by a bee. You didn't just grit your teeth and carry on. Not even close.

I reached into the glove compartment and touched the gun. It was cold, like death.

I picked it up.

It was heavy, just like the gun my father had let me hold and fire.

It was real.

I looked through the windshield and saw Ted turning around. He wasn't holding his cell phone to his ear anymore. He was walking toward the car.

I slammed the glove compartment shut.

Ted got into the car and replaced his cell phone in the holder mounted on the dashboard.

I sneezed.

"Bless you," Ted said. He glanced at the glove compartment. "I wish I could offer you a tissue, but I'm all out."

"No problem," I said.

I should have told my mother about the gun. I came close to it a couple of times — once that night over supper and again the next morning while she was getting ready to go to work. But both times I ended up keeping my mouth shut. My reasoning: I knew that my mother liked Ted a lot. I knew that she was thinking about marrying him. And I knew that if I told her I had found a gun in his glove compartment, she would freak out, and that would make things between her and Ted tense at a time when Ted was already stressed. I decided that I would tell my father instead, as soon as he got back from Switzerland. He would be calm about it. He would have a talk with Ted. He would find a way to make him get rid of the gun. And, if Ted was lucky, he wouldn't get into any trouble on account of it. In retrospect, though, I shouldn't have waited. I should have told my mother. If I had, things might have turned out differently.

* * *

Ted dropped me at Morgan's house, but Morgan didn't want to stay at home when the malls were open and before the January sales ended for another year. So we went shopping. Several hours later, we dropped our bags (half a dozen large ones for Morgan, one small one for me) in a booth at our favourite coffee place and reviewed our purchases — actually, Morgan gloated over hers one by one.

"Is this a bargain or what?" she said, holding up a soft pink sweater that she had scored at seventy-five percent off the regular price. "It's perfect for a cottage vacation in March, don't you think?" She grinned. I stared at her.

"I haven't said yes yet."

Morgan groaned. "Come on, Robyn. Tell Ben we'll go. Please. He described the place to me. It sounds amazing. It has seven bedrooms, Robyn. Seven. And a hot tub. You are so lucky to have a boyfriend like Ben. Rich *and* generous. We'll have a great time. Please?" She made puppy eyes at me.

"I don't know," I said.

"You don't have to be head-over-heels in love with him, Robyn. I'm not asking you to make a life-long commitment. But think what a great time we could have. I've seen some of those places from the water — they're spectacular. Wouldn't you like to check out what they're like inside? Even Billy is excited — apparently there's a conservation area nearby 'where you can see horned owls." She shook her head as if she couldn't imagine why that was such a big deal. "Everyone wants to go, Robyn."

Everyone, it seemed, except me.

It was hot in the coffee shop. I peeled off the sweatshirt I was wearing over a long-sleeved T-shirt.

Morgan frowned. "Hey, what's that?"

"What's what?"

Instead of answering, she reached across the table, grabbed the two hearts dangling from the chain around my neck — I had forgotten I was wearing it — and pulled them toward her for a closer look. She examined them critically.

"I guess being rich doesn't mean you have the best taste in jewellery," she said dismissively.

"It's supposed to be the thought that counts," I said. I tried to hook the chain away from her.

Too late.

She had flipped the hearts over and was reading

the inscription on the back. She shook her head and looked across the table at me like I was a hopeless case.

"I should have known," she said. "Ben would have chosen something more elegant. And more expensive."

"Well, I like it," I said. I yanked the hearts out of her hand and tucked them back inside my T-shirt.

"If you like it so much, how come I've never seen it before?" Morgan said.

I avoided her eyes. I hadn't told her about Nick's gift — I hadn't told anyone except Ben, who had been there when I'd opened it — because I knew she would do exactly what she was doing now: she would disapprove.

"Does Ben know you're wearing tacky jewellery that another guy gave you?" she said. "And why *are* you wearing it, anyway? I thought you'd given up on Nick. He abandoned you, Robyn."

"He called me."

"Nick?" She looked incredulous. *"Nick* called you?"

I nodded.

"And? Is he back? Where was he? Did he tell you why he took off?"

"It's complicated," I said.

Morgan studied me for a moment. "He's not back, is he?" she said.

"I don't know."

"What do you mean, you don't know? You just said he called you."

"He called from out west somewhere," I said.

"What's he doing there?"

"I don't know." I felt like screaming the words. I didn't know. I didn't know anything because no one had bothered to tell me. I explained that I had dropped the phone and accidentally deleted the message.

"What did he say?" she asked.

I repeated his words as well as I could remember and told her that there had been a noise that had drowned out all but a few of them: *coming back* and *love* and *call.* Morgan shook her head.

"For all you know, Robyn, he could have been calling to tell you that he's not *coming back* even though he'd *love* to and that's why he decided to *call.*"

"Thanks a lot," I said.

"Well, it's true. You said you could only make out a few words."

I hated to admit it, but she was right.

"Has he called you since then?" she said.

"No."

"Come on, Robyn. Get real. You don't know where he is. You don't know what he actually said. And he hasn't called you back. Doesn't that tell you something?"

"It's only been two days," I said. "He'll call. I know he will." At least, I *prayed* he would.

"Maybe you should face facts," Morgan said. "Nick took off without a word — while you were out of town. He's been gone for nearly two months now — "

"It's only been six weeks."

Morgan sighed. "You can't keep pining for him, Robyn. You have to move on. Besides, Ben is a better person for you. He's considerate. He's reliable. He's rich. That's the kind of guy you deserve — " She broke off suddenly and looked over my shoulder. "Ben alert!" she hissed.

I turned and saw Ben and Billy coming through the door of the coffee shop. They were scanning the place, looking for us. I grabbed my sweatshirt and quickly pulled it on again.

"What are they doing here?" I said.

"Billy did a shift at the drop-in centre this morning." It was Billy who had talked me into volunteering there before Christmas. "I told him we'd probably stop off here after we finished shopping. Ben must have been there, too."

They spotted us.

"Surprise!" Ben said as he dropped down beside me, forcing me to slide over in the booth to make room for him. "I still have that surprise for you," he whispered before kissing me lightly on the cheek. "So, how were the shopping wars?"

"We got some great bargains," Morgan said. "Didn't we, Robyn?"

"Yeah? Let's see," Ben said.

Morgan beamed at him. She adored Billy, but Billy would never in a million years have asked to see her purchases. He had no interest in shopping. She handed a bag across the table to Ben. It slipped out of his hands. Something fell out of it and onto the floor. I automatically ducked down to retrieve it. When I straightened up, Ben was staring at me. Actually, he was staring at my neck. So was Morgan. I glanced down. When I bent over, Nick's chain had slipped out from under my sweatshirt. I started to tuck it back in, but Ben caught it in his hand and turned it over. He stared at it for longer than it should have taken to read the inscription.

"Why are you wearing that?" he said.

I glanced at Morgan, who immediately shifted her eyes down to the tabletop. Billy looked confused. He opened his mouth to say something, but closed it again when Morgan elbowed him. I looked into Ben's angry eyes. Should I answer him truthfully — I'm wearing it because I miss Nick? Should I refuse to answer — after all, what business was it of his? Or should I lie?

In the end, I said nothing.

"This is the necklace that guy sent you, isn't it?" he said. "The one you said I didn't have to worry about."

"Ben, I'm sorry. I just — " Just what? I glanced at Morgan again, but her face was blank. She liked Ben. She didn't want to get involved, especially if it meant hurting his feelings.

"I'm crazy about you," Ben said. Morgan's eyes popped wider at that. "I've told you that." Morgan was staring at me, no doubt wondering why I had kept *that* piece of information from her, too. "And you never said anything that led me to think that you felt differently." He broke off and flicked the entwined hearts with one finger. "He's why you don't want to come up to the cottage, isn't he?"

"Ben, I'm sorry. I care about you. Really I do. It's just that — "

He waited, but I couldn't find the right words.

"Just that what?" he said finally, his voice soft now despite the hurt look in his eyes.

"He called me. Nick called me."

"Is he back?"

"No. At least, I don't think so. But hearing his voice . . . I need time to think, Ben." I looked at the bruised expression on his face and wondered if Ted had looked like that when my mother had said more or less the same words to him last fall. But I couldn't help it. I *did* need time. I *did* need to think.

Ben stood up slowly.

"You know how to get in touch with me," he said. He bent and brushed his lips against my cheek. "I really do care about you, Robyn."

Morgan sighed as she watched him go.

"He's so sweet," she said. "I think you're making a big mistake, Robyn. Ben is the guy for you."

I glanced at Billy, but all he did was shrug — his way of telling me that it was up to me.

I wished I knew what to do.

Chapter 10

It had been quiet all week. Nick hadn't called again. Part of me wanted to believe that maybe Morgan was right, maybe I'd been reading the wrong message into the few words I'd been able to make out from his phone call. That was easier than thinking the alternative: that Nick had been waiting for me to call him. He'd sounded a little hurt that I hadn't already been in touch with him. But how could I have been? I'd searched his apartment and had found no clue about his whereabouts. I had talked to his aunt. I'd tried to track down any friends who might know where he was. But if he had given me a phone number in his message, it had been drowned out with the rest of his words, and if he didn't realize what had happened, he would probably assume that I was mad at him or that I didn't care about him anymore. And if that happened, what were the chances that he would swallow his pride and call me one last time? Knowing Nick, they were practically nil.

Ben didn't phone, either, but he did send me a little ceramic pot of flowers — forget-me-nots. I couldn't help smiling when I unwrapped them. Maybe Morgan was right about him, too. Maybe he was the one for me. He was thoughtful and even-tempered, and, boy, was he patient.

Ms Denholm was all dimples and smiles at the front of the class. She looked more relaxed than she had in days. Maybe that was because Ted was spending a lot of time with her. He seemed determined to make her feel safe. He cooked supper for her one night. He took her to a foreign film festival. She seemed to enjoy his attention. If she was still worried about Mikhail Mornov, she was hiding it well.

My father was still in Switzerland. One of the entertainment shows on TV did a news item about the upcoming wedding of the famous drummer and even more famous TV actress, and I was sure I saw my father standing in the background.

My mother was five days into a trial that she told me was going to last at least a couple of weeks, which meant that she was putting in long hours reviewing testimony and preparing what she was going to say. She spoke to Ted every day and seemed to think everything was going well.

The school play was into rehearsals.

"Has everyone who's going on the trip handed in their signed permission forms?" Ms Denholm said after rehearsal on Friday. She had arranged for the cast and crew of the school play to take a behind-the-scenes tour of a local theatre, after which we were going to watch a dress rehearsal. I had signed up. So had Billy. So had Keisha Minotte. And so, therefore, had Morgan. She kept close to Billy whenever Billy was anywhere near Keisha or Ms Denholm.

That day after rehearsal, Ted was waiting to pick up Ms Denholm. He was taking her out to dinner. I was in the school atrium, almost at the main doors. I looked out and saw her get into Ted's car. She leaned over to him and kissed him on the cheek before they drove away. I shouldered my backpack and headed for the bus stop across the street.

I didn't see him until I was on the bus. Mikhail Movnov. Even then, I wouldn't have spotted him if I hadn't looked out the rear window. He was standing near the cedar hedge that ran along one side of the school and he was looking back at the main door of the school. I thought he must be waiting for Ms Denholm. But if he'd been standing there when I left the school, he would have seen her with Ted. Then I saw him raise his hand, as if he were greeting someone. But who?

The bus turned the corner. The school disappeared.

Chapter 11

The day at the theatre was fascinating. I'd had no idea how much activity there was behind the scenes. Everyone had a great time — well, everyone except possibly Morgan, who was annoyed when Keisha settled in on one side of Billy to watch the dress rehearsal. Morgan looped her arm possessively through Billy's as soon as the curtain went down and announced that she was treating him to dinner at his favourite vegan restaurant. Billy beamed at her. He's a beanpole who is almost always hungry.

"What about you. Robyn? Do you have plans for dinner?" Ms Denholm said.

"Well, no."

"I was wondering if you'd like to have dinner with me — not as your teacher, but as Ted's daughter. I gather that he and your mother are, well . . . Ted speaks very highly of her and from what he says, it seems we have a good chance of being related one day. Maybe we should get to know each other. What do you say?"

What could I say?

"I do a pretty good spinach soufflé," she said a little later, as she unlocked the door to her apartment. "And a decent salad with a boiled salad dressing — one of my mother's recipes."

"I thought soufflés were hard to make," I said.

"Not if you know what you're doing. I'll show you. I'll make some tea to have while we work."

She handed me an apron and put on the kettle. It wasn't long before she was whisking up a salad dressing.

"We'll need six eggs for the soufflé," she said.

I checked the fridge.

"You only have four."

"Oh no." She thought for a moment. "Do me a favour, Robyn? Run across the hall and ask Nat for some."

She wanted *me* to go and ask her neighbour for eggs?

Ms Denholm must have sensed my hesitation.

"Don't worry," she said, stirring the dressing. "She doesn't bite."

"It's not that. It's just that, well, I don't know her."

Ms Denholm laughed. "Of course you do," she said. "It's Nat. Natalie Rachlis. The art teacher. She lives across the hall."

Oh.

I knew that Ms Denholm and Ms Rachlis were friendly at school, but I hadn't known that they lived in the same place. Then I remembered the day that Ted and Mikhail Mornov had got into that fight. I'd seen Ms Rachlis nearby. I wondered if they had become friends because they not only taught at the same school but were also neighbours.

I crossed the hall and rapped on the door to the rear apartment. An eye clouded the peephole. A moment later the door opened.

"Robyn," Ms Rachlis said. "Melissa said she was inviting you over. What can I do for you?"

"Ms Denholm was wondering if she could borrow two eggs."

"Sure. Come on in."

The layout of Ms Rachlis's apartment was similar to the layout of Ms Denholm's, but Ms Rachlis's place wasn't nearly as nice. Clothes and papers were strewn all over the furniture in the living room. A table in one corner of the kitchen was heaped with paints and paper, canvases and brushes. A computer sat at one end of it, with a printer on the floor below it. Dirty dishes were stacked in the kitchen sink. The floor looked as if it hadn't been washed or even swept recently. Ms Rachlis's feet made a crunching sound as she walked across it and opened the refrigerator door. She rooted around inside.

"I know I have some eggs in here somewhere," she said. She pulled out a jar of pickles, a container of milk, another of yoghurt, some mustard, some cheese . . . "Ah," she said triumphantly. "Here they are." She produced an egg carton. I wondered how long it had been in there.

Her telephone rang. She went over and looked at it.

"Telemarketer," she said. "The machine can get it."

Sure enough, after three rings, her answering machine clicked on and we listened to the pre-recorded voice of a man advertising a carpet-cleaning service.

"What did I tell you?" Ms Rachlis said. "Some days telemarketing calls are the only calls I get. I come home and see the little light flashing on my machine. I think maybe it's someone calling to ask me out. I hit the Play button. And what do I hear? Five or six calls from people offering to clean my chimney, my carpets, my furnace, you name it."

I couldn't help thinking that she should accept a few of those offers.

"If you had voice mail, you could delete the messages as soon as you hear it's a telemarketer," I said.

"The phone company charges you a monthly fee for that service," Ms Rachlis said. "My mother gave me this old machine when I left home. It's practically an antique, but it works like a charm — for free. My motto is, if it ain't broke, keep working it. Here you go." She handed me the eggs.

I was thanking her when something started thumping on the floor beneath my feet. I glanced at Ms Rachlis, who rolled her eyes.

"Mrs. Wyman," she said. She grabbed a set of keys from her messy kitchen table and headed for the door. I followed her and almost tripped on a baseball bat that was lying in her hall. She scooped it up and propped it beside the door. "A girl needs protection in the big city," she said.

Just then Ms Denholm appeared in the hall, holding a wooden spoon.

"Oh," she said when she saw Ms Rachlis. "I was just going downstairs to see what she wanted."

"I'll take care of it this time," Ms Rachlis said. "You can get the next one."

"Good luck," Ms Denholm said. "I hope that whatever she's looking for this time doesn't turn out to be something she gave away ten years ago."

Ms Rachlis rolled her eyes again.

Ms Denholm just laughed. "One time the two of us spent a whole evening looking for . . . what was it, Nat?"

"A porcelain bullfighter that she said she bought in Spain before the Second World War."

"That's it," Ms Denholm said. "We looked everywhere, but we couldn't find it. Finally Mrs. Wyman called her son, who lives out west. It turned out that she had given the bullfighter to one of her nieces ten years ago. Her son sent us each a basket of fruit after that. He said he appreciates everything we do."

"Translation: he doesn't want us to leave because it might not be so easy to find such accommodating tenants to replace us," Ms Rachlis said.

* * *

We ate the soufflé and salad, which were as delicious as Ms Denholm had promised, and chatted about English and drama and school — and Ted.

"Do you think they're really going to get married?" Ms Denholm said.

"I don't know," I admitted. "But he's a great guy,

and I know my mom really likes him. So do I."

We were cleaning up the dishes when the phone rang.

Ms Denholm answered it. I didn't pay any attention until I heard her say, "Stop calling me! Stop calling me!" in a shrill and panicked voice.

I spun around to look at her. Her face was paper-white. She was still holding the receiver, but her hand had dropped to her side.

"Ms Denholm?" I said.

"It was him," she said. "But how did he get through to me? My number is unlisted."

I wondered if my father would have any doubt about her claims of being stalked if he had seen the look on her face.

"Are you okay?" I said.

She stared at me.

"Do you want me to call the police?"

She shook her head slowly.

"How about if I call Ted, then?" I said. "Maybe he could — " I stopped abruptly when I heard footsteps in the hall. Ms Denholm froze. Someone knocked on the door. Ms Denholm seemed to be holding her breath. I tiptoed to the door and looked out through the peephole.

"It's Ms Rachlis."

Ms Denholm nodded feebly, and I unlocked the door.

"Sorry to interrupt," Ms Rachlis said, "but *I'm* out of coffee and I have a long night of marking ahead of me. I was wondering if I could borrow — " She took in the expression on Ms Denholm's face. "Melissa, what's wrong? What happened?"

"The phone," Ms Denholm said. "He called."

"Who called?"

"Mikhail. He got my number somehow and he called."

Ms Rachlis's face clouded. She glanced at me.

"I was just going to call her father," I said. "He'll know what to do."

"Good idea," Ms Rachlis said. She got Ms Denholm to sit down while I phoned Ted.

"What did he say to her?" he said, after I'd explained the situation.

"I don't know."

"Tell her I'll be right there. And Robyn? Tell her to keep the door locked."

I said I would. Then, because it was worth a try, I dialled *69 to see if I could find out the last number that had called. Instead, I got the same recorded message I got when I'd tried to return Nick's call. Whoever had just called Ms Denholm had used a pay phone.

* * *

Ms Rachlis had succeeded in calming Ms Denholm down a little by the time Ted got there. But Ted was jittery.

"Did you call the police?" he said.

Ms Denholm shook her head.

"They won't do anything," she said. "He didn't break any law. He didn't even say anything. He hardly ever says anything."

Ted glanced at me. I don't think I imagined the fleeting look of doubt in his eyes.

"Are you sure it was him?" he said. "Maybe it was a wrong number."

Ms Denholm shook her head. "It wasn't a wrong number, it was Mikhail. I know it was. He wanted to let me know that he has my number. No matter how many times I change my number, he always finds out."

"Pack a bag," Ted said. "You're staying with me until this is settled."

"I couldn't do that," Ms Denholm said.

"Melissa, I insist. This man knows where you work. He knows where you live. Now he knows your phone number. Don't tell me you feel comfortable with that."

"You should go, Melissa," Ms Rachlis said. "You'll be safe."

Ms Denholm didn't answer.

"Pack a bag," Ted said, his voice gentle now. "I'm taking you to my place and that's final. I have plenty of room. And an unlisted phone number."

"*I* have an unlisted number," Ms Denholm said.

"Melissa, I live in a secure building," Ted said. "There's a guard on duty twenty-four hours a day and video surveillance at all the entrances. Natalie is right. You'll be safe there. We'll figure out what to do. I promise."

"But my car . . . " She had rented one while she waited for the final settlement from her insurance company.

"You don't need your car."

"How will I get to and from school without it?"

"I'll drive you until we get this all cleared up."

But she insisted, and finally Ted relented. "I'll take you to my place in my car now," he said. "Once I know you're safe, I'll take a cab back here and pick up your car. Okay?"

Ms Denholm nodded. She went into the bedroom to gather her things. Ted turned to me and handed me his car keys.

"I'm parked around the back, Robyn. Why don't you wait in my car? We'll drop you at the bus on the way."

I knew he wanted to talk to Ms Denholm alone, so I agreed. As soon as I got into Ted's car, I checked the glove compartment. The gun was gone.

Chapter 12

I opened my locker at lunchtime and took out the little gift box that I had found tied to my locker door that morning. It contained a heart-shaped key chain. The enamelled heart was decorated with — what else? — forget-me-nots. I showed it to Morgan. She eyed it critically until I said, "It's from Ben." Then she broke into a smile.

"It's so cute," she said. "Does that mean you two are back together again?"

"I don't know," I said. I hadn't spoken to Ben since the restaurant.

I was sure Morgan was going to ask if I'd heard from Nick, but she didn't. She also didn't tell me — *again* — what a great guy Ben was and how he was perfect for me. In fact, she surprised me by saying nothing at all. She just watched in silence as I tucked the key chain into my pocket

I fingered it after school that day as I watched the actors rehearsing the play onstage. Then I felt the chain around my neck. I still hadn't decided what to do.

It was obvious that Ben wasn't angry with me. He cared about me, and he kept going out of his way to let me know it.

And Nick? What had he done? He still hadn't called me back.

I dug my cell phone out of my bag and stepped out of the school auditorium to make a call. I returned to my seat in time to see Ms Denholm flip her cell phone shut and turn to Ms Rachlis, who was sitting beside her, overseeing the set-design team as they painted sets.

"That was Ted," she said.

"I understand completely why you're staying with him," Ms Rachlis said. "But I sure do miss you, Melissa. Mrs. Wyman is driving me crazy. She's been hammering on the ceiling almost non-stop since you left. I think she watches at the window until she sees my car. The moment I let myself into the apartment, she starts pounding. If I don't get down to her place right away, she hobbles up the stairs and pounds on the door. It wasn't so bad when there were two of us. But now it's just me."

"I wish this would end," Ms Denholm said wearily. She sounded tired and discouraged. "I want things to be back to normal — whatever that is."

My cell phone rang. My heart skipped a beat. My hand trembled as I reached for it. But it wasn't the caller I'd been hoping for. It was Ted.

"I need a favour, Robyn," he said. "I just called

Melissa to let her know that I'm tied up in a meeting that I can't get out of. Would you go back to my place with her and stay until I get there? She's been so nervous lately."

I knew my mother would be working late, so I said yes. When I told Ms Denholm, she shook her head.

"I think Ted is more nervous than I am," she said. But she didn't try to talk me out of going with her. "We'll have to take a taxi. I don't have my car with me."

Although Ted had taken Ms Denholm's car back to his place as she'd asked, he had insisted on driving her to and from school every day.

"I'll give you a lift," Ms Rachlis said.

"Are you sure? It's out of your way."

Ms Rachlis made a face. "Let's see . . . should I take my best friend where she wants to go, or should I rush home and let Mrs. Wyman drive me crazy? Tough decision." She laughed. "I'll meet you back here in fifteen minutes. I need to get some things from my classroom."

She was back when she said she would be and we all got into her car and drove across town to Ted's place.

"I've heard about this building," Ms Rachlis said as she pulled into the condominium's driveway. "I've always wanted to see what it looks like inside. And from the way you described it the other night — "

Ms Denholm looked at me and blushed. "I called Nat to let her know where she could reach me. I told her about Ted's place."

"It really is nice," I agreed. "Ted has great taste."

"You're more than welcome to come up and see, Nat," Ms Denholm said.

Ms Rachlis parked in the visitors' parking area and we took the elevator up to the main floor. Ms Denholm led the way to the security desk where a guard — not Darren, this time — greeted her with a smile. He became more formal when he asked Ms Rachlis and me to sign the visitors' log. We rode the elevator up to the penthouse floor. Once again Ms Denholm led the way, this time to Ted's door. She fished in her purse for her keys and unlocked first one deadbolt, then another. I didn't remember there being two deadbolts on Ted's door. He must have had the second one installed recently. Ms Denholm pushed open the door and stepped inside. I followed her. Behind me I heard Ms Rachlis say, "What's this?"

Ms Denholm and I turned around and looked back at Ms Rachlis, who was still out in the hall. She bent over to pick something up. It was an envelope. She frowned at it as she straightened up.

"It's for you, Melissa," she said.

She held the envelope out to Ms Denholm. Ms Denholm's name was typed on the front of it, but there was no address on it and no stamp.

"Where did it come from?" Ms Denholm said.

"It was sticking out from under the mat," Ms Rachlis said, gesturing to the rectangular welcome mat on the floor in front of Ted's door.

Ms Denholm's fingers trembled slightly as she opened the envelope and pulled out a folded piece of paper. Her face turned white when she read it.

"Melissa, are you all right?" Ms Rachlis said.

Ms Denholm handed her the note. Ms Rachlis read it. Her expression grew grim.

"What's the matter?" I said. "What does it say?"

Ms Rachlis looked at Ms Denholm, who was still staring at the sheet of paper. Ms Rachlis handed it to me. It looked like it had come off a computer printer. It said, *If I can't have you, no one will.* There was no signature. I don't know what my father would have thought, but the shattered look on Ms Denholm's face convinced me.

"You have to call the police," I said.

Ms Denholm shook her head slowly. "They won't do anything. They won't be able to prove it was him. They won't be able to stop him. No one can stop him."

"But he's threatening you," I said. "You can't let him get away with it."

Ms Rachlis looked nervously up and down the hall.

"How did he get in here?" she said. "This is supposed to be a secure building. That guard downstairs must have been asleep on the job."

Ms Denholm's face turned a sickly shade of grey. If Mikhail Mornov had got past the security guard . . . She glanced up and down the hall, her eyes wide and searching. Then she slammed the door, locked both deadbolts, and attached the security chain.

"Please let me call the police," I said.

Ms Denholm didn't answer. She kicked off her boots and threw off her coat. Ms Rachlis and I took off our coats and boots, too.

"How does he even know where you're staying?" Ms Rachlis said.

"He must have followed me."

"Or Ted," I said. "I saw Mikhail outside of school on Friday. I'm pretty sure he saw you and Ted leave together."

I regretted my words as soon as they were out of my mouth. Ms Denholm's face lost all of its colour. She looked at the note again.

"He's telling me he knows where Ted lives," she said. "He's never going to leave me alone."

She walked quickly through the living room and down the hall that led to Ted's guest room. When she came back, she was holding a gun. I'm no expert, but I was pretty sure it was the same one that I'd seen in Ted's glove compartment. Ms Rachlis did not look surprised when she saw it.

"What are you going to do with that, Melissa?" she said.

"Protect myself."

"If you want protection, you should call the police," I said.

"They never do anything," Ms Denholm said. She looked at Ms Rachlis. "Remember all those phone calls?" Ms Rachlis nodded. "He always called from a pay phone, always when he knew I was home. I hooked up a tape recorder to my phone — I have it hooked up again." I had thought the machine that was attached to her phone was an answering machine, like Ms Rachlis had. But I'd been wrong —

it was a tape recorder. "But he never says anything that I can play for the police. It's always just dead air. Remember last time, Nat? I wrote down all the times he had called and I gave the police that information. They said that at least half the time, he had an alibi — he was at work or he was with someone who swore that he hadn't been near a phone."

Ms Rachlis nodded.

"Usually it was a family member," Ms Denholm added. "The police always believed them."

"And those things he used to leave at my door or near my car — remember, Nat?" She shuddered. "Headless dolls. One time a doll with its chest ripped open and fake blood all over it and a note that said, *Heartless.*"

"Just like the flowers you got at school," I said.

She nodded. "Another time, he left a dead cat at my door."

Just like her stepfather had done to her mother.

"But there are never any fingerprints. Never anything that proves it was him."

I kept staring at the gun. Ms Rachlis caught the look on my face. She put out her hand.

"Give me that thing," she said. "Let me put it away for you."

The phone rang.

Ms Denholm jumped.

"It's probably Ted," I said.

Ms Denholm picked up the receiver and said hello. Her face turned grey again as she listened. Her voice was shrill when she said, "How did you get this number?" But before whoever it was could answer, she slammed down the receiver. Her hand was shaking. She was still gripping the gun.

"Melissa, what's wrong?" Ms Rachlis said.

The phone rang again.

"Melissa?"

"It was him," Ms Denholm said. "It was Mikhail. Why doesn't he leave me alone?"

The phone stopped ringing, but just for a minute. Then it started again.

"You should get out of here," Ms Rachlis said.

"You should call the police," I said.

"You should just go somewhere far away," Ms Rachlis said. "Ted can help you. He's well off, Melissa. He can help get you settled somewhere far away from here. You can change your name again."

"Just like my mother did," Ms Denholm said. She stared at some distant memory.

The phone rang again, jarring her back to the here and now. We all looked at it. I grabbed the receiver and said hello.

"Melissa?" said the voice at the other end of the phone.

"Melissa isn't here," I said. "We're phoning the police. Don't call here again."

"Please don't hang up," the voice said. "Tell her I love her. Tell her that I just want to talk to her before she marries — "

I slammed down the receiver.

Ms Denholm was trembling.

"What did he say?" she asked.

"That he loves you. That he — "

Her knees buckled. She grabbed the back of a chair for support. Ms Rachlis put an arm around her to steady her.

"Melissa, you have to get away. You're not safe here anymore," Ms Rachlis said. She looked around nervously, as if she expected Mikhail Mornov to walk through the wall. "The sooner you leave and the farther away you go, the better. I'll pack your things and get them to Ted so that he can send them to you once you decide where to settle. I'll tell Patrick Wyman that you had a family emergency and had to leave town. I'm sure he won't have any trouble getting someone else to rent your apartment. I'll even help him."

Ms Denholm's eyes were glazed with tears. Slowly she straightened up and said, "You're right. I have to get out of here. But where can I go? I don't know anyone."

"You can check into a motel for now," Ms Rachlis said.

Ms Denholm shook her head. "Even if you pay cash, they take a credit-card imprint."

"Melissa, he can't check every motel in the area. He won't find you — not before you've decided where you're going."

"He always finds me," Ms Denholm said. "James" — I was pretty sure she meant James Duguid, the man her mother had married — "always boasted how easy it was to find people. That's why my mother refused to have any credit cards. She didn't even have a bank account. It's even easier to track people down now, with so much information stored in computers and accessible to hackers who know what they're doing."

Her voice was flat, as if she were resigned to the fact that there was no place for her to hide. If I'd had any doubts about Ms Denholm's version of events, they had vanished. She was clearly terrified.

Then I had an idea.

"We can go to my house," I said. "He doesn't know where I live."

"That's a good idea, Melissa," Ms Rachlis said.

Ms Denholm shook her head. "He's been in the building," she said. "What if he's down there somewhere, watching? What if he follows me?"

"Your car is here, isn't it?" Ms Rachlis said.

Ms Denholm nodded. "It's in the parking garage."

"That's it, then. We'll make sure he doesn't," Ms Rachlis said firmly. She thought for a few moments. "You and Robyn will take your car. I'll take mine. You leave the parking garage first and I'll follow you. When you get to the street, turn right. I'll turn left and circle around the block so that if he's there — *if*, Melissa — he'll think that we've gone our separate ways. But I'll catch up with you and stay a safe distance behind you until we're sure no one is following you. If someone is following you, I'll stay with you. If you're not being followed, I'll flash my headlights so that you can relax. Then I'll go back to the house and start getting your things together quietly. You and Ted can work out where you're going, and Ted can pick up your things. You don't even have to tell me if you don't want to. The important thing is that you'll be safe. Okay?"

Ms Denholm drew in a deep breath as she considered this suggestion. "Okay," she said finally. "Just let me get my things."

"I'll help you," Ms Rachlis said. "And, please, put that gun away."

Ms Denholm nodded distractedly.

"Maybe I should call Ted," I said.

But Ms Denholm had already made up her mind. "We'll call him from the car," she said.

She and Ms Rachlis went to the guest room together. I heard their voices. They were arguing about the gun. Ms Denholm wanted to take it with her. Ms Rachlis wanted her to leave it behind. Finally Ms Rachlis got her way and they came back into the living room. Ms Denholm was carrying the same small suitcase she had taken with her when Ted insisted that she stay with him.

We put on our coats and boots. Ms Denholm hunted in her pocket for something, but didn't find whatever she was looking for.

"My keys," she said.

"I saw them in the bedroom," Ms Rachlis said.

Ms Denholm ducked back through the living room and down the hall to the bedrooms. While we waited for her, I said, "The first thing she should do is call Ted and the police. She can show them the note. They'll have to listen to her."

Ms Rachlis disagreed. "The first thing she needs to

do is put as much distance as possible between herself and Mikhail," she said.

Ms Denholm hurried back into the foyer clutching her keys.

"Let's go," she said.

The elevator arrived.

Ms Denholm still looked nervous, but she got into the elevator and let Ms Rachlis press the button for the ground floor. She caught her breath and held it when the elevator finally stopped on the main floor and the doors parted. Ms Rachlis got out first and looked around. She beckoned to us. We got out. Ms Denholm looked around apprehensively. Apart from the security guard, there was no one in the lobby. We hurried to the elevator that would take us down to the visitors' parking area. I glanced at the security guard while we waited for it. He was looking at Ms Denholm.

"I'm going to ask the guard if he let anyone go up to Ted's place," I said.

"We don't have time," Ms Rachlis said. "Melissa should get out of here right now."

The elevator doors opened.

I looked back at the security guard again and told myself that he would have to wait. First we would get Ms Denholm to safety. Later I'd get Ted to talk to him. If the police wanted proof that Mikhail Mornov was stalking Ms Denholm before they did anything, maybe the guard could help provide it. Maybe Mikhail Mornov had talked him into letting him into the building. Maybe he had used some kind of ruse.

Or maybe one of the security cameras had caught him sneaking in.

The elevator doors opened in the basement. Ms Denholm gasped. A man was standing a few metres away in the shadows. Ms Denholm slipped her hand into her pocket. The man slammed a car door and stepped into the light. He was at least sixty years old and was carrying a suitcase. He nodded pleasantly at us as he waited for us to step out of the elevator. Ms Denholm relaxed a little. We found her car.

"Wait until you see me behind you," Ms Rachlis said. "Then drive out of the garage and stop when you get to the road. As soon as you see me in your rear-view mirror, turn right. I'll turn left and catch up to you. Don't worry, Melissa. You're going to be fine."

Ms Denholm hugged Ms Rachlis.

"Thank you, Nat," she said. "Thank you for everything. I don't know what I would have done without all your help."

"All I want is for you to be safe," Ms Rachlis said. "You'll get through this. I know you will."

Ms Denholm and I got into her car and buckled our seat belts. As soon as we spotted Ms Rachlis's car, Ms Denholm backed out of her parking space. She drove to the garage doors and held her breath again when the door started to roll up automatically. She scanned the exterior for any cars with people in them. We both did. But neither of us saw anything. The circular driveway in front of the building was deserted.

We headed for the main road.

I turned and watched for Ms Rachlis's car. It didn't emerge from the parking garage until Ms Denholm had pulled up at the stop sign where the condominium driveway met the road. Even then, Ms Rachlis's car hung back. Only after we had made a right turn did she pull forward to the stop sign and flip on her left-turn signal. She disappeared from sight. I turned to look out the rear window of Ms Denholm's car. There were a couple of vehicles behind us. One, driven by an old man, passed us quickly. Another, a Volkswagen, stayed behind us. I stared at it nervously until I saw that a middle-aged woman was driving it. She was alone. When we got to the next intersection, she signalled a left turn. We continued going straight. As we cleared the intersection, I saw Ms Rachlis's car swing onto the road behind us.

As we travelled the next several blocks, other cars pulled onto the road behind us or passed us, but no one seemed to be following us — except for Ms Rachlis. After a kilometre or so, Ms Denholm said, "Nat just flashed her headlights. That means we're in the clear."

"I'm going to call Ted," I said. Ms Denholm didn't argue with me. I hunted in my purse for my cell phone. It trilled before I could punch in Ted's number. I checked the display screen. My heart pounded in my chest as I pressed the On button and said hello.

"I got your message," the voice on the other end said. I was surprised by how good it felt to hear it.

"Ben, I'm sorry," I said. I glanced at Ms Denholm. "I miss you," I said quietly.

"I miss you, too." Ben's voice was sweet and warm. "I want to see — " His voice faded.

"What?" I said. "Ben I can't hear you. I'm on my way home — " There was silence on the other end. "Ben? Ben?"

Nothing. Maybe he was having trouble with his phone. I pressed the Off button and waited for a few moments. Nothing. I punched in Ben's number. It went straight to voice mail. With a sigh, I tried Ted's number and got his voice mail. I tried his office number. A woman answered and told me that Ted was in a meeting and couldn't be disturbed. I said it was urgent. She promised to get a message to him as soon as she could. A few minutes later, my phone trilled again. This time it was Ted. I told him what had happened.

"Where are you now?" he said.

"On our way to the house. We thought she'd be safe there for a while."

"Did you check to make sure you're not being followed?"

I reassured him that we had.

"Okay," he said. "As soon as you get home, go inside, lock the door, and call me so that I know you're safe. I'll be there as soon as I can. You're on your cell, right, Robyn?"

I said I was.

"Keep it clear in case I need to get hold of you, okay?"

I said I would and set my phone in the cup holder between the front seats, where I could grab it quickly if I needed it. I told Ms Denholm what Ted had said. Then, because I was still spooked by the gun, I asked her about it.

"My mother bought it from a man whose house she cleaned," Ms Denholm said. "She was so scared. She wanted to be able to protect herself — and me."

"I saw Ted with a gun."

She nodded. "When he found out I had it, he took it away from me."

Well, that explained what I had seen in Ted's glove compartment. I was glad that it was safely back at Ted's place.

We drove the rest of the way in silence. Ms Denholm checked the rear-view mirror obsessively. Other than that, she seemed lost in thought. She slammed on the brakes when we were two doors down from my house.

"There's a car in front of your house," she said, pointing. "And there's someone in it."

I peered at the vehicle.

"It's Ben. He's my . . . " I hesitated. "My boyfriend," I said at last. It sounded right.

Ms Denholm let out a long breath. She eased her car into my driveway. I looked back at the street. Ben was getting out of his car.

"Come on, Ms Denholm," I said. "Let's go inside. We'll call Ted and let him know we're here."

Ms Denholm was staring at the windshield. Finally she shook her head.

"I can't keep running," she said. "My mother spent her whole life looking over her shoulder. She was terrified of what would happen if James ever found her. She made herself sick worrying about me. She worked at menial jobs because those were the only kind she could get that would pay her cash. We never had anything. We never went anywhere. If she'd had her way, I would never have gone to university." Her voice became quiet. "I never would have met Mikhail." She stared straight ahead for another few moments. Then she said, "I refuse to live like that."

"You don't have to," I said. "We'll go inside. We'll call Ted. And my mother. She's a criminal lawyer. She'll know what to do. Please?"

Finally, distractedly, she nodded. Relieved, I got out of the car. As soon as I did, Ben started toward me. I glanced at Ms Denholm. She hadn't moved.

"I've been waiting for you," Ben said. He slipped an arm around me. It felt good.

Ms Denholm's car started to move backward, down the driveway.

"Wait!" I said.

The car stopped and the passenger-side window whirred down.

"I'm not going to spend my life running," she said. "The police keep telling me there's nothing they can do without proof. I have to go back."

"Ms Denholm, wait!"

"What's going on?" Ben said.

Ms Denholm hit the gas. Her car shot backward,

cleared the driveway, and disappeared around a corner.

"She's going back to her place," I murmured. Not only was it possible that Mikhail would be waiting for her there, but that seemed to be what she wanted. What had she said? *The police keep telling me there's nothing they can do without proof.* It sounded to me like she was hoping to confront him so that she could provide that proof. But what if he hurt her? What if he did worse?

"Robyn, what's the matter?" Ben said.

"We have to catch up with her, Ben. Come on."

"I don't understand."

"I'll explain. Come on."

I grabbed his hand and we ran to his car.

"Where are we going?" Ben said as he pulled away from the curb.

"To Ms Denholm's place. Where we saw the fight."

He nodded. A few moments later we were on the main road, travelling as fast as traffic and the speed limit would allow.

"Robyn, about last week . . . "

Ted. I had to call Ted and let him know what had happened. I groped in my bag for my cell phone. It wasn't there. Then I remembered. I had left it in Ms Denholm's car.

"Where's your phone, Ben?"

"What?"

"Your cell phone. I need to make a call."

"It ran out of juice," he said. "That's why we got cut off. I have to recharge it."

"Great." I scanned the road ahead of us but didn't see any sign of Ms Denholm's car. Maybe she'd taken a different route home. Maybe she wasn't going home at all. Maybe she was going back to Ted's place. I wished I had my phone. "Faster, Ben."

"I'm going the speed limit, Robyn. And you still haven't told me what's going on."

I filled him in on what had happened.

"So this guy really is stalking her?" He sounded like he had doubts.

"It sure looks like it. And now I'm afraid she's going to do something stupid. She told the police about him, but they've never been able to prove anything."

"But if he did all those things, there must be some evidence," Ben said. "Unless this guy is some kind of criminal mastermind."

"He sounds pretty smart," I said. "And Ms Denholm knows it. I think she's tired of no one believing her. I'm afraid she's going to confront him. I'm afraid she's going to make him do something so that the police can arrest him."

"What do you mean, make him do something?" Ben glanced at me. "You don't think she's going to put herself in danger, do you?"

"I don't know for sure," I said. "But, yes, I think she might."

"We should pull over. We should call the police," Ben said.

He was right. But then he said, "Hey, is that her car?"

The car immediately in front of Ben's was a little red Mini. Right in front of that was Ms Denholm's car.

"Keep up with her, Ben," I said. "If we stay with her, we can stop her from doing anything stupid when she gets home."

For the next twenty minutes, I strained to keep sight of Ms Denholm's car. Ben stayed a steady car length or two behind her all the way, and I began to think that everything would be okay. Wherever she ended up, we'd be right there with her. I'd be able to persuade her to come with us or to call the police. No one would get hurt.

Ms Denholm turned abruptly, without signalling her intent. That caught Ben off guard. He missed the turn and had to take the next right and circle around the block. My heart raced the whole time. Then I spotted her turning into the driveway of the big house where she lived. She disappeared behind it.

After that, everything happened so fast that it was hard to digest. By the time it was over, Ms Rachlis was in shock, Mikhail Mornov lay dying in the snow, and Ms Denholm was holding a gun that she had just fired. Not much later, I was at the police station, giving a statement.

Chapter 13

Detective Charlie Hart found a room where we could talk in private.

"Where's Ben?" I said.

"Another detective is talking to him."

I wasn't surprised. The first police officers on the scene had separated us — Ms Denholm, Ms Rachlis, Ben, and me. They didn't want us talking among ourselves, comparing stories, and influencing each other, either consciously or unconsciously.

"Is he okay?" I said. He had seemed so calm, down on his knees in the snow behind Ms Denholm's house, his coat off despite the cold, his attention one hundred percent focused on what he was doing. I lost track of him after the ambulance arrived.

"He seems to be," Charlie Hart said. "He's a level-headed kid, huh?"

I nodded.

"What about you, Robyn? How are you doing?"

"What?" I was thinking about what had happened,

about what I had seen and done.

"Most people, when they see something like that, they have a reaction," Charlie Hart said. He peered into my eyes. Maybe he thought I was having a reaction. "Are you okay?"

I nodded.

He looked at me a little longer before he said, "I know you already told the officers at the scene what you saw," he said. "But I understand you were with Melissa Denholm for most of the afternoon, so I need to go over it again with you. I need you to tell me everything that happened. Okay?"

"Okay," I said.

I started from the beginning — again. I told him why Ben and I had gone to Ms Denholm's house. I told him that we had arrived right after she did.

"When Ben pulled around the back of the house, she was just getting out of her car," I said. "She started to walk to the back door — "

"The back door?"

"Ms Denholm's and Ms Rachlis's apartments are on the top floor of the house. You get to them through a door at the back of the house. There are stairs that go directly to the top floor."

Charlie Hart nodded. "So you saw her heading for the back door. Then what?"

"Then I heard shouting from somewhere inside the house."

"What do you mean, shouting?"

"Two people were yelling at each other. A man and a woman."

"Did you hear what they were saying?"

I shook my head.

"But it sounded like they were fighting," I said. "Then I heard a crash."

"A crash?"

"Like something heavy had been dropped or thrown. Ms Denholm must have heard it, too, because she stopped and looked up. So did I. I saw a face at the window."

"Which window?"

"Up on the third floor. It was one of the windows in Ms Rachlis's apartment. Her apartment is at the back of the house. Ms Denholm's apartment looks out over the front."

"The face you saw, do you know whose it was? Did you recognize it?"

I shook my head. "It happened too fast. It was only there for a second or two. All I know for sure is that the lights were on in the apartment and someone looked out. But I couldn't make out who it was. Then I heard more shouting. Then a thumping sound. It got louder and louder — like someone was running down the stairs."

"What about Melissa Denholm? What was she doing while this was going on?"

"She was standing near the back door, but she backed away when she heard the thumping. For a minute it looked like she was going to go back to her car. I think she was scared."

"What makes you say that?"

"She *looked* scared," I said.

"What happened next?"

"I heard someone scream. It was Ms Rachlis. She screamed, 'He's got a knife. He's going to kill me.'"

Charlie Hart leaned in close when I said that.

"She said he had a knife?"

I nodded.

"And you heard her say he was going to kill her?"

"Yes. And he was shouting, too."

"He? Mikhail Mornov?"

"Yes. He was shouting something, but I couldn't make out what it was because Ms Rachlis was screaming so loud. She came running out through the door. It looked like she was bleeding here." I touched the left side of my forehead.

"It was pretty dark back there, Robyn," Charlie Hart said.

"I saw her face when the back door opened. There was a light on in the stairwell." He nodded. "Then the man — Mikhail Mornov — ran out of the house right behind her."

"Did you get a good look at him?"

"I got a good enough look to know it was him. I'd seen him before. But after he and Ms Rachlis ran out of the house and the door closed behind them, it was dark. There weren't any lights."

"Did you see if he was carrying anything?"

He meant, did I see if he was carrying a knife? I shook my head.

"It was too dark. But after — " I had to blink back the picture that flashed before my eyes. "After he was shot, I saw a knife lying on the ground beside him."

"Then what happened, Robyn?"

I closed my eyes so that I could visualize the sequence of events.

"Ms Rachlis screamed at Ms Denholm to help her. She said that he had a knife and that he was trying to kill her. That's when Ms Denholm shot him."

"Ms Denholm shot Mikhail Mornov?"

"Yes."

"Do you know where she got the gun?"

"It used to belong to her mother. She had it for protection. Ted took it away from her."

"You mean her father, Ted Gold?"

"Yes. He took it away from her. I thought she'd left it at his place like Ms Rachlis told her to."

"Tell me about the shooting," Charlie Hart said.

"When Ms Rachlis ran out of the house bleeding and screaming that Mikhail Mornov was trying to kill her, Ms Denholm took the gun out of her pocket. At first she just stood there. I didn't think she was actually going to use it. Mikhail Mornov was chasing Ms Rachlis and she was running toward Ms Denholm and screaming. Ms Denholm shot him."

"Do you remember how many times she fired the gun?"

Did I ever. How do you forget something like that?

"Five times." She didn't hit him all five times. She hit him twice. He hadn't been far from her when she fired. I'd seen his hands reach out, as if he were going to slash at Ms Rachlis or maybe attack Ms Denholm. That's when she shot him. "She fired the gun five times."

"And then what happened?"

"We just stood there for a few minutes. I think we were all in shock." I know I was. At least, that's what I told myself. "Except for Ben. Ben tried to help him."

Ben had dashed to where Mikhail Mornov was lying, dropped to his knees, and pulled off his gloves. He reached out. I caught my breath, imagining that Mikhail Mornov would rise up, grab the knife again, and stab Ben, just like in a suspense movie. Ben pressed two fingers against Mikhail Mornov's neck, feeling for a pulse. He must have found one because he tore off his jacket, folded it quickly, and pressed it hard against Mikhail Mornov's chest.

"Find a phone," he said to me, his voice eerily calm in contrast to the jumble of emotions and images that were cascading through my brain. "Call 911. Then come back here and help me. He has a head wound, too."

I didn't move. I couldn't.

"Robyn," Ben said, his voice louder and firmer, but still calm. "Call 911."

I stood where I was, staring down at Mikhail Mornov and at the blood pooling in the snow. I said, "He tried to kill her, Ben."

The look he gave me filled me instantly with shame.

"He needs help, Robyn. If he doesn't get it, he's going to die."

Even then, he had to ask me a third time before I staggered to Ms Denholm's car, retrieved my cell phone from the cup holder between the seats, and made the call.

175

I didn't tell Charlie Hart all of that, but I wondered if Ben had told the police officer who had taken his statement. I also wondered what Ben had thought when I'd stood there, frozen and unwilling to help. I wondered what he thought of me now.

"Like I said," Charlie Hart said, "he seems like a level-headed kid. The ambulance guys said they don't think Mornov would be alive if it weren't for that young man."

"Is he going to . . . is he going to be okay?" I said.

Charlie Hart shook his head. "I understand it doesn't look good." He shifted a little in his chair. "Did anything else happen before the police arrived?" he said.

"What do you mean?"

"After Ms Denholm shot Mikhail Mornov, before the police arrived, did anyone — Ms Denholm or Ms Rachlis, for example — say anything or do anything?"

I thought for a moment.

"Ms Rachlis told Ms Denholm that Mikhail Mornov showed up at her apartment. She said he cornered her in her kitchen and tried to force her to tell him where Ms Denholm was. He said he'd kill her if she didn't tell him. She said he hit her. I guess that's why she was bleeding. She said when she saw Ms Denholm's car, she knew she had to warn her."

"She said she saw Ms Denholm?" Charlie Hart said.

"Yes. So I guess it must have been Ms Rachlis's face I saw at the window. She said she tried to get away from him and was running downstairs to warn Ms Denholm, but that he chased her and he had a knife and he said he was going to kill her."

"Do you remember her exact words?"

I closed my eyes to visualize the moment. "She said, 'Melissa, he wanted to kill me. He wanted to kill both of us.'"

"What about Ms Denholm? Did she say anything?"

"No. She just dropped the gun and stood there and watched Ben trying to help Mikhail Mornov." She had looked at the knife, too. "It looked like she was in shock. Then the police arrived."

Charlie Hart looked across the table at me. "Is there anything else, Robyn? Anything at all that you remember?"

I shook my head.

* * *

My mother was sitting in the lobby of the police station. Ted was beside her. They both looked tired and tense. My mother stood up when she saw me. She rushed toward me and hugged me.

"Are you all right?" she said.

I nodded. "Where's Ben?"

"He left about ten minutes ago."

"He did?" I had been hoping that he would be waiting for me. He wasn't. What did that mean? I thought again about how I had just frozen whereas Ben had sprung into action. "Did he say anything?"

My mother shook her head. Ben probably thought I was a horrible person for not immediately calling for help. He probably wondered how I could be so heartless. My mother hooked a finger under my chin and made me look her in the eyes.

"How are you doing? You were there when it happened. You saw everything. Are you okay?"

I nodded. "I'm okay. Ms Denholm didn't have any choice, Mom. He was attacking Ms Rachlis."

My mother shook her head. "We're not going to talk about it here, Robyn," she said, sounding one hundred percent like a lawyer. She led me over to where Ted was sitting. He stood up.

"Are you okay, Robyn?" he said.

I nodded. "Where's Ms Denholm?"

"The police are questioning her," my mother said. She turned to Ted. "I'm going to take Robyn home."

"Of course," Ted said. "I'm going to wait for Melissa."

They were two parents, acting like two parents.

My mother put a hand on Ted's arm.

"Call me," she said. "I don't care how late it is, call me. I want to know that she's home safe with you."

Ted kissed her lightly on the cheek. He didn't say anything.

* * *

My mother drove us home. Neither of us spoke on the way. I don't know what she was thinking about, but the evening's events kept playing over and over in my head. Anyone who had ever doubted that Ms Denholm was being stalked would have to believe her now. Mikhail Mornov had threatened Ms Rachlis with a knife. Ben and I had seen it. If Ms Denholm hadn't shot him, he might have killed Ms Rachlis.

Then he might have killed Ms Denholm. I kept wondering, What would have happened if Ms Denholm hadn't decided to go back to her apartment? Would Ms Rachlis have told Mikhail Mornov that Ms Denholm had gone to my house? Then what? What if she had refused to tell? Would he really have killed her? Or what if Ms Denholm had arrived home five minutes later? Would Ms Rachlis still be alive? Over and over it went in my head, all those questions, and then the chaotic scene behind the house — the shouting, the running, the screaming, the gunshots. Ms Rachlis, Ms Denholm, Mikhail Mornov, Ben. The police.

My mother made hot chocolate. She was a big believer in the power of warm milk. It would calm me and help me get to sleep, she said. But once I was home, I couldn't sit still and, in contrast to my silence in the car, I couldn't stop talking. I told my mother what I had told Charlie Hart. I told her what I had seen — I described for her, frame by frame, the movie that kept playing in my head. And then, just like that, I burst into tears. I was having what Charlie Hart would have called a reaction. I told her what Ben had done and what I had said. My mother hugged me and held me and told me I was going to be okay. She said it was a shock to see something like that and that it could really throw a person. She said I shouldn't worry, that she was sure Ben understood. I couldn't tell whether she believed that or not.

"What about Ms Denholm?" I said when I had calmed down a little. "What do you think is going to happen to her?"

"From what you described, it sounds as though she shot him because she thought he was going to kill Ms Rachlis, and that she also had good reason to fear for her own life."

"Will they charge her with anything?"

"There's a strong case for self-defence," my mother said. "But I gather the gun she had was unregistered. And then there are issues about its transportation and use . . . We'll have to see, Robyn."

"What if he dies?"

My mother looked even more solemn. "We'll cross that bridge when we come to it."

I went up to my room, but I couldn't sleep. I couldn't read, either. I couldn't make myself concentrate. I heard the phone ring and crept to my bedroom door to listen. From the soft tone of my mother's voice, I guessed she was talking to Ted. She was on the phone for a long time. Afterward she came upstairs to go to bed. On the way to her room, she pushed open my door.

"You're still awake," she said, surprised. "Do you have any idea what time it is?"

I glanced at the clock on my bedside table. It was nearly three in the morning.

"I can't sleep," I said.

"I'm not going to the office tomorrow," she said. "I'm going to work here instead. I think you should stay home from school."

"What did Ted say? What happened with Ms Denholm?"

"They haven't charged her with anything yet.

Ted's not sure if they're going to or not. He said the detectives he talked to seemed sympathetic, but they told him they were still investigating and that they wanted to talk to Mikhail Mornov if and when he regains consciousness. He said they appeared to give a lot of weight to what you and Ben told them." She sighed. "Sometimes I wish life were like television, but it isn't. It will take time. We'll just have to wait and see."

Chapter 14

Morgan showed up at my house after school the next day and demanded that I dish up the details.

"You have to promise you won't tell anyone else," I said. "My mother and Ted would kill me if they knew I was talking about it."

"I promise," Morgan said. "But I can tell Billy, right?"

"Yes, you can tell Billy," I said, because, unlike Morgan, Billy wouldn't dream of sharing the information with anyone else.

Morgan swore a solemn oath, and I filled her in.

"Wow," she said. "Little Miss Denholm actually pumped lead into a guy?"

"She saved Ms Rachlis's life."

"I know. But, wow, I can't believe it."

"I was there and I can hardly believe it," I said. We talked about it a little longer. Then Morgan said, "What's up with you and Ben?"

"What do you mean?"

"I mean, the last I heard, you were doing a Patricia and telling him you needed more time. The next thing I hear, he happens to arrive at your house just in time to get you to Ms Denholm's place, where you witness Ms Denholm saving Ms Rachlis from Ms Denholm's psycho ex-boyfriend. How did that happen? Was it a coincidence?"

"I called him from school," I admitted. "I wanted to thank him for all his gifts and to ask him to call me — if he still wanted to."

Morgan beamed. "Finally came to your senses, huh?"

I didn't know what to say. I had been thinking about Ben almost non-stop since the shooting. What if I hadn't called him? What if he hadn't called me back? What if his cell phone hadn't conked out on him and he hadn't been at my house when I got there with Ms Denholm? I wouldn't have been able to go after her. I would have had to call someone instead — Ted or my mother. Or the police. Maybe this time the police would have believed that Ms Denholm was in danger and would have gone to her house to check on her. Maybe if they had, Ms Denholm wouldn't have had to shoot Mikhail Mornov.

Or maybe it would have turned out the way that Ms Denholm had predicted. Maybe the police wouldn't have sent anyone because they wouldn't have believed her. After all, Mikhail Mornov had had an alibi for when Ms Denholm's car was trashed. And it was Ted who had thrown the first punch in his altercation with Mornov. So then things would have ended just as they did, with Mikhail Mornov threatening Ms Rachlis and Ms Denholm having no choice but to shoot. The only difference would have been that, without Ben there to perform first aid, Mikhail Mornov would have died.

"What's the matter?" Morgan said, frowning at me. "You called Ben. He showed up. That means you two are back together, right?"

"I don't know," I said. "We didn't have much chance to talk, and I haven't heard from him since last night." I was too afraid to call him, too afraid of what he might be thinking of me. Instead, I had been waiting for him to call me. The longer my phone went without ringing, the more convinced I became that he had changed his mind about me.

"Call him, Robyn. Talk to him," Morgan said. "A guy like that isn't going to wait forever."

I knew she was right. I wondered if it was already too late.

As soon as Morgan left, I punched in Ben's cell phone number. He didn't answer. I left him a message: *Call me. Please.*

Five minutes later my phone rang. My mouth went dry. My heart pounded. But it wasn't Ben. It was my father.

"What's this Vern tells me about Melissa Denholm shooting someone?"

"Where are you, Dad?"

"I'm still in Switzerland. Are you okay, Robbie? Vern tells me you were there when it happened."

"How does Vern know that?" I said. Then, "Never

mind. Stupid question. Yes, I was there. So was Ben."

"What happened exactly?"

I told my father what I had told Charlie Hart.

"So everyone is okay?" my father said.

"Apart from Mikhail Mornov, I think so," I said. "The police haven't charged Ms Denholm with anything, but I think Ted is worried that they will. Mom keeps telling him that no news is good news. She had to do what she did, Dad. He had a knife. He was chasing Ms Rachlis. I keep wondering what would have happened if Ms Denholm hadn't got there when she did."

"Looks like my antennae were off this time," my father said. He asked me a few more questions. He also asked me about a dozen times if I was sure I was okay. Then, probably to change the subject, he told me about the wedding. "You wouldn't believe how much money they're spending on this thing, Robbie." Before he rang off, he said, "I'm flying back on Saturday night. How about brunch on Sunday? We can catch up."

"Won't you be tired, Dad?"

He laughed. "I'm never too tired for you, Robbie. See you Sunday."

* * *

Ben phoned me that night.

"I'm sorry I didn't call sooner," he said. "Things have been kind of crazy around here. While I was waiting for you to finish talking to the cops, I called home. I wanted to let Catherine know I was going to be late. She was freaking out because couldn't get in touch with my father. He's out of the country on business."

"She was so worried about you that she was freaking out?" I said. Nothing Ben had ever said about his stepmother had led me to think she would do something like that.

"She wasn't worried about me," Ben said. "She was in labour. You wouldn't believe how fast I ran out of the police station when she told me. I had to flag down a cab because my car was still at Ms Denholm's place. I took Catherine to the hospital. Robyn, I was with her when everything happened. It was amazing. I have a baby sister. You should see her. She's so tiny. And so cute."

I congratulated him.

There was a brief silence on the other end of the line.

"Are you okay?" Ben said finally. "You sound kind of funny."

"I — I thought you were mad at me," I said.

"What for?" He sounded astonished.

"For what I did. You know, when you told me to call an ambulance."

"I'm not mad at you, Robyn. You were in shock. It wasn't your fault."

Relief flooded over me.

"Well, *you* were amazing," I said. "Charlie Hart told me that if it hadn't been for you, Mornov might have died."

"That first-aid training really kicks in when you need it," Ben said modestly. "So, how about we get together tomorrow night?"

"I can't," I said, and hoped he heard the disappointment in my voice. "Now that all of this is over, my mother and Ted want to do a sort of family get-together with Ms Denholm. Hey, do you want to come?"

"It sounds like something the four of you should do together, without any outsiders," he said.

"How about Friday night?"

"I've got a few family things of my own, both Friday and Saturday," Ben said. "Because of the baby. How about Sunday?"

I thought about the brunch date I had made with my father, but I knew he would understand.

"Sunday is perfect," I said.

"I'll pick you up at ten. We'll grab some breakfast and then maybe go skating. Do you like to skate?"

I imagined Ben holding my hand as we circled the rink.

"I love it," I said. "I'll see you then."

Chapter 15

THURSDAY, FEBRUARY 11

I went back to school. So did Ms Denholm. Everyone was talking about what she had done – it wasn't every day that a teacher shot someone – but Ms Denholm acted as if she didn't notice. She called Billy aside before the play rehearsal and told him that he might have to hold off on sets for a couple of days. Ms Rachlis wasn't coming back to school. Ms Denholm had been told that there would be a new substitute art teacher by Monday. "She'll be able to advise you," she said.

* * *

The dinner was Ted's idea. Because of everything that had happened since my father had found Ted's daughter for him, my mother hadn't had much opportunity to get to know Ms Denholm. Ted thought it would be nice if we all spent an evening together.

The phone rang just as my mother and I arrived. Ted answered it, but didn't say much.

"That was Melissa," he said. "She's running a little late. A reporter was waiting for her outside her house. She's refused to answer her doorbell and her phone number is unlisted, so they have no choice but to camp out on her doorstep if they want to talk to her. So far they've stayed away from the school, but I gather that's because the principal read them the riot act. They've been calling me, too. At the office — not at home. Thank goodness for unlisted phone numbers."

He took our coats and then showed us into the living room. He poured a glass of wine for my mother and a soda for me and then sank down onto the sofa beside my mother.

"You look exhausted, Ted," she said.

"I am," he admitted. "I want this whole nightmare to be over. The police still haven't said what they're going to do. They're waiting to question him — " He meant Mikhail Mornov, but couldn't bring himself to speak his name. " — if he regains consciousness. If he doesn't . . . " His voice trailed off and he looked plaintively at my mother.

"They have Natalie Rachlis's statement," my mother said. "The man was attacking her with a knife. They have Melissa's statement. And Robyn and Ben were there. They witnessed the whole thing. I doubt they're going to charge Melissa. It was self-defence, Ted."

"Do they think he's going to recover?" I said.

Ted shook his head. "He's still critical," he said. His expression was unusually sombre. "I know this sounds callous, but in a way, I almost hope he doesn't. That way, this whole thing will be over for Melissa. She'll have one less thing to worry about."

I caught the look on my mother's face even if Ted didn't and knew right away what she was thinking: If he died before the police had a chance to talk to him, maybe Melissa would have one more thing to worry about.

"The police haven't been able to figure out how he got into the building to leave that note," Ted said. "The guard didn't see him. There are security cameras at all the entrances and exits, but they didn't pick him up, either. Some of the condo members wanted cameras on every floor, but that was voted down. I voted against it. I thought it was too much like Big Brother. Now I'm not so sure." He shook his head. "Melissa tells me he's a very clever man. He must be if he got in and out of this building without being seen. I asked them if they found any fingerprints. That would prove to them once and for all that he was stalking Melissa. But they won't tell me anything."

"They never do," my mother said.

The buzzer rang twenty minutes later. Ted went to the intercom by the door. He poked his head back into the living room a moment later.

"She's on her way up," he said.

A few minutes later, the doorbell rang.

"I tried to talk Nat into coming with me," Ms Denholm said from the foyer, while Ted helped her off with her coat. "I thought it would do her good to be

190

around people. I'm worried about her. She's quit her job. She refuses to leave her apartment. She's leaving town this weekend."

"Before the matter is resolved?" my mother said, surprised.

"She spoke to the police. They have her statement and she promised to keep them informed of her whereabouts, in case they need to ask her anything else," Ms Denholm said. "She says she can't sleep. She keeps remembering what happened."

"A change will probably do her good," my mother said. "Sometimes that's the only way to put a bad experience behind you. How are *you* doing, Melissa?"

"I'm fine," Ms Denholm said. "Well, as fine as I can be under the circumstances."

I wondered if she kept playing the incident over in her head the way I did. I kept hearing the screams, seeing the knife, recoiling at the sound of the gunshots. For her it must have been a thousand times worse. She had decided to confront her nightmare. She had gone back there. She had saved Ms Rachlis and stopped Mikhail Mornov. But it must have occurred to her that the end result could just as easily have been much different, and that must have shaken her — badly.

She managed a wan smile.

"At least I don't have to look over my shoulder," she said. "I'm grateful for that. But I'd like it to be over once and for all."

"Let's pretend it *is* over, just for tonight," Ted said. "We won't think about it. We won't talk about it.

We'll just try to have some fun."

And we did.

Gourmet cooking is one of Ted's hobbies. We ate — five courses in all — and talked and even laughed. I could tell from what my mother said and the way she looked at her that she liked Ted's daughter. And when I said, "Ms Denholm, could you please pass me the pepper?" Ms Denholm said, "Please, call me Melissa, at least when we're not at school."

After dinner, Ms Denholm announced that she would clean up.

"Oh, no," Ted said. "That can wait."

"I insist," Ms Denholm said. "After everything you've done . . . " She reached across the table and touched his arm. "It's the very least I can do . . . Dad."

Ted's eyes got misty when she called him that. She squeezed his arm. He beamed at her.

"I'll help you," I said. I got up and began to clear the table.

"You two relax," Ms Denholm said to Ted and my mother. "We'll be done before you know it."

We carried the dishes into the kitchen. Ms Denholm rinsed them and I stacked them in the dishwasher.

"I'm sorry about Ms Rachlis," I said as I worked.

"So am I," Ms Denholm said. "I'm even sorrier that she feels so guilty about what happened."

"Guilty? It wasn't her fault."

"You don't know Nat," Ms Denholm said. "She blames herself. It's because of her that I met Mikhail."

That was a surprise. It must have shown on my

face because Ms Denholm laughed.

"Nat's a good friend. I met her during my last year at university," she said. "We did our teacher training together. Shortly after I accepted the job I have now, Nat told me that she was looking for something out this way. I spoke to the principal about her. Then, when the art teacher had that accident, Nat got the job. She's terrific. She's been so supportive. But she keeps saying that if it weren't for her, Mikhail wouldn't be in my life. I was so introverted back then . . . I don't know if Ted told you about my stepfather — the man my mother married after she left Ted."

"He told me a little," I said. Actually, it was my father who had told me, but I wasn't sure how she would feel if I admitted that.

"He turned out to be a real psycho," she said. "He never wanted to let my mother out of his sight. He was awful to her — and to me — whenever I was supposed to go and see Ted. I used to be afraid to go — I worried what James might to do to my mother if I left her alone with him."

I thought about Ted picking her up for a visit when she was eight years old. He said she'd cried every night. Now I knew why.

"When my mother finally left him, he went crazy," she continued. "He broke into her car. He broke into the house so many times I lost count. She complained to the police, and they always went and talked to him. But they never had enough evidence to arrest him for anything. They told my mother there was nothing they could do. Finally, in the middle of the night, we moved. My mother changed our names and spent the rest of her life looking over her shoulder. She was so scared that she bought a gun from a man whose house she cleaned. After all that . . . well, I guess you could say I was cautious around guys."

I could just imagine.

"By the time I was doing my teacher training, James — my stepfather — had died. But my mother was sick and everything was so hard. I was miserable. Nat decided I needed cheering up, so she dragged me to a party. And that's where I met Mikhail. I was so nervous. He seemed nice, but I kept remembering my mother telling me how nice James had been when she first met him, and how much he had changed as time went on. I was afraid — what if Mikhail turned out to be just like James?" She looked at me and shook her head. "That must sound kind of paranoid to you."

"No, it doesn't," I said.

"But Nat knew him, so I thought it would be okay. And he really did seem nice. And gentle."

"Did you tell him about what had happened to your mother?"

"No. Mostly I avoided talking about that." She put the last couple of dishes into the dishwasher and closed the door. "I can see now that my mother was right. It's so easy to be taken in by men like James Duguid and Mikhail. Even I didn't pick up on the warning signals."

"What do you mean?"

"My mother warned me about guys who act like

you belong to them and them alone before you really know them. Mikhail was like that. He got serious so fast. When he found out how I felt about smoking, he quit — that was on our second date."

"When I saw him outside school, he had a cigarette in his hand."

Her smile was sour.

"He couldn't let go of them, either," she said. "He always fiddled with them. Sometimes he even put one in his mouth. But he never lit them — not around me, anyway. He kept telling me he'd do anything for me and that he never wanted to let me out of his sight. It scared me. Then he proposed to me. I'd only known him for a few months."

"That's pretty fast," I agreed. But Ben had made up his mind about me pretty quickly, and I was one hundred percent positive that he wasn't a stalker or abusive.

"When Nat found out I was seeing him, she tried to warn me," Ms Denholm said. "She knew him from before. She'd heard a few things." She sighed. "She keeps saying she should never have insisted that I go to that party."

After we finished in the kitchen, we all played cards and laughed some more. It felt good to see everyone so happy — and to see Ted so obviously delighted to be with his daughter. It wasn't until much later, when I was lying in my bed at home, that I thought about Ted's phone number. Like Ms Denholm's, it wasn't listed in the phone book. Yet Mikhail Mornov had managed to get both numbers.

He'd called Ms Denholm at her apartment and at Ted's condo. Ms Rachlis had been right to warn Ms Denholm about him — he was very clever and, from the sound of it, very sinister.

Chapter 16

"I'd offer to go with you," Morgan said. "I know the best places for baby clothes."

This was news to me.

"Since when?" I said. "Who do you even know who has a baby?"

"Billy's sister is pregnant. I've been looking around, for when the time comes."

"Leanne is *pregnant*?" This was also news to me.

"She just found out," Morgan said. "She hasn't told anyone yet except for family."

"Now you're *family*?"

"Well, I *am* Billy's girlfriend," she said. "I wanted to tell you, Robyn, but Leanne wants to be sure first. You know."

I wanted to be understanding, but I couldn't help feeling left out. Billy and Morgan had been my best friends since forever. We told each other everything. It felt strange that the two of them knew something but had kept it from me.

"I'd go with you, Robyn. But Billy and I are leaving right after school."

More news.

"Leaving for where?"

"Billy promised ages ago that he'd attend this big conference on birds. He's supposed to make a presentation about DARC."

"And *you're* going with him?"

She blushed. Tough-as-nails Morgan actually blushed. "The conference starts tonight and runs right through till Sunday afternoon," she said. "It's Valentine's Day on Sunday. It wouldn't feel right if we weren't together."

"Together . . . talking about dead birds," I said. "Sounds like the perfect Valentine's Day to me."

"I really love him, Robyn."

"Uh-huh. I don't suppose Keisha Minotte is going to be at this conference, is she?"

Morgan's expression hardened. "So what if she is? I'm going because I want to be with Billy. Is that a crime?"

"I'm sure you'll have a great time," I said. "You and all those bird people. Ben and I are getting together on Sunday, too. I'd like to find something for his baby sister before then."

Morgan grinned at me.

"You're doing the right thing," she said. "He's a great guy."

* * *

On my way to my locker after school, I ran into Ms Denholm. She was coming out of the art room carrying what looked like a heavy box.

"Do you need some help with that?" I said.

She shook her head.

"I think I can manage. I'm just taking this down to the car. I'm helping Nat clean out the art room. Tomorrow we're packing up her apartment. She's leaving as soon as we're done. But I bet Nat could use some help." She ducked her head into the room. "Couldn't you, Nat?" she called cheerily.

Ms Rachlis didn't answer.

"She's having a tough time," Ms Denholm said in a quiet voice. "If you wanted to pitch in, I know she'd appreciate it." When I nodded, she said, "Go on in. I'll be right back."

Ms Rachlis was emptying her desk drawers, packing some items into a cardboard carton and tossing others into a wastepaper basket. She was pale and looked thinner than the last time I'd seen her. She had obviously been deeply affected by what had happened.

"What can I do?" I said.

She looked blankly at me for a moment. "Those brushes," she said. "They need to be cleaned. I want to leave everything tidy for the next teacher."

I set to work. Ms Denholm joined me when she returned. When we had cleaned all the brushes, she turned to Ms Rachlis.

"Are you almost ready?" she said.

Ms Rachlis nodded.

"I'm taking these two boxes," she said. "This one is garbage."

Ms Denholm and Ms Rachlis each picked up a box of the things Ms Rachlis wanted to keep. The third box was filled with discarded paper. I volunteered to empty it into one of the recycling bins at the end of the hall.

"If you need help tomorrow, I'm available," I said. Billy and Morgan were going to be out of town and Ben was tied up with family business. "I have a few errands to do, but I can come over after that."

"That would be great, Robyn. Thanks," Ms Denholm said as she and Ms Rachlis headed for the stairs. "We'll see you then."

I carried my box to the recycling bin and tipped out all of the scrap paper — old newspapers that had been torn into strips for papier mâché, stacks of magazines with holes in the pages where pictures had been cut out for art assignments, pages covered with preliminary sketches and designs . . . some of the drawings were pretty good. I reached in and pulled out a couple of sheets that were covered with sketches of little bunches and arrangements of flowers, some gathered together with ribbon, some in vases, some held in the arms of cuddly teddy bears. They were terrific. I wondered if a student had done them or if they were Ms Rachlis's work. Ms Denholm had said she was talented. If these were her sketches, Ms Denholm was right.

Chapter 17

"Well, good morning," my mother said when I walked into the kitchen to make some tea and toast. She looked radiant in the morning sun that was streaming through the window.

"Morning," I said. "Morning, Ted." He was sitting at the table beside her, holding one of her hands. Neither of them made any attempt to conceal it or to break contact with each other.

"Ted and I were thinking of taking a drive up north," my mother said. "We thought we'd do some cross-country skiing. Do you want to come?"

"I have plans," I said. Plans that did not involve watching my mother and Ted get all mushy with each other.

"We should be back by suppertime," my mother said.

"Unless we stop off at that little restaurant I was telling you about," Ted said. "The one with all the fireplaces." He squeezed her hand. My mother giggled.

"We'll be back when we're back," she said. "What are you going to do all day?"

"I'm going to go shopping this morning," I said. "Then . . . "

But my mother wasn't listening. She was looking at Ted again, and she had a big, goofy grin on her face. I didn't bother to finish my sentence. I wondered if there had been any change in Mikhail Mornov's condition, but decided that if there had been, someone would have told me.

* * *

I went to the store that Morgan had recommended, picked out a pink and yellow outfit for Ben's baby sister, and had it gift-wrapped in teddy-bear wrapping paper with a big pink bow. Next to the baby store was a shop that sold hand-dipped chocolates. I bought a heart-shaped box for Ben.

Ben.

Not Nick.

It felt right. Ben was here. He was doing everything right. Nick wasn't even around. I thought about the words of an old song my father liked, something about loving the one you're with. Well, why not?

I wrote out a card, slipped it into a little envelope on which I printed Ben's name, and attached it to the ribbon on the box. With both my purchases in a bag, I hopped the bus and rode it to Ms Denholm's place.

* * *

Ms Denholm — *Melissa* (I had to keep reminding myself that outside of school, she was Melissa and that she might one day be my stepsister) — and Ms

Rachlis were getting out of Melissa's car when I arrived at their house. Melissa smiled and waved me over.

"You're just in time," she said. "We've got a lot of boxes to fill."

Ms Rachlis nodded at me. She still looked thin and pale, and her hair hung in greasy strings. I felt sorry for her.

"Nat is leaving first thing in the morning. We're packing her things so that I can ship them back home for her." She glanced at the bag I was carrying. "You can leave your things in my apartment if you want, Robyn." She circled around to the trunk of the car and opened it. It was filled with what looked like a dozen or more cardboard boxes nested inside each other. She and Ms Rachlis must have scrounged them from a supermarket. Melissa took half of them and gave me the other half.

"Nat's going to supervise," she said in a cheery voice. "You and I will be her helpers."

We went upstairs. I dropped my purse and my purchases in Melissa's apartment, but kept my cell phone with me in case Ben called. I closed Melissa's door and crossed the hall to Ms Rachlis's apartment. If anything, it was even messier than it had been the time I'd gone to borrow eggs. There were boxes everywhere, some of them sealed and neatly labelled with their contents, others heaped high with Ms Rachlis's possessions, and others that looked as though Ms Rachlis had just scooped up armfuls of items — shoes, boots, books, painting supplies — and dropped them willy-nilly inside.

"We've got the kitchen under control," Melissa said. "Nat, why don't you pack the bedroom? Robyn, you can tackle the bookshelves in the living room. I'll take care of the knick-knacks. Don't worry, Nat. I'll wrap everything in newspaper so that nothing gets broken."

Ms Rachlis disappeared into the bedroom. I followed Melissa into the living room.

"I'm glad she's getting away from here," she said to me in a soft voice. "She's taking an extended vacation. She told me she might even look into a teaching position overseas for a while. She needs to be able to forget about what happened."

I couldn't imagine what it must have been like for her to have been face to face with Mikhail Mornov and have her life threatened. Once again I found myself wondering what would have happened if Melissa hadn't decided to go home — or if she hadn't taken that gun with her.

"If you hadn't shown up when you did . . . " I began, but I stopped when Ms Rachlis appeared in the doorway. She looked at me, but all she said was, "I need another box." She picked up an empty one and disappeared back into the bedroom with it.

Melissa and I set to work. I packed books — art books, poetry books, novels — while Melissa wrapped vases, figurines, and framed photographs, carefully packing them between layers of crumpled newspaper. As I set the last of the books into a box, Melissa tossed me a roll of silver-coloured tape.

"You can use this to seal the box," she said.

"Duct tape?" I said.

Melissa laughed. "Nat calls it her secret weapon. It's strong. And you can use it for all kinds of repairs. One time we were going out and the hem of my dress came down in the back. Nat taped it up with a few pieces of duct tape. It held for the whole night."

I sealed the box and wrote *Books* on the side in marking pen.

"Once we get everything in here packed, I'll vacuum," I said. The carpet was filthy. I wondered how long it had been since someone had run a vacuum cleaner over it. One spot beside an over-stuffed armchair was covered in . . . what was that, anyway? It looked like tiny shreds of brown paper. I looked more closely and picked up a few pieces with my fingertip. Tobacco — at least, that's what it smelled like. I frowned. I had never seen Ms Rachlis with a cigarette and, so far, I hadn't seen any ash-trays.

"Let me help you with that, Nat," Melissa said.

I looked up. Ms Rachlis was coming out of the bed-room with two boxes stacked one on top of the other.

Thump.

I jumped.

Thump-thump.

It was coming from the floor and it startled me. It must have startled Ms Rachlis, too, because she lost her grip on the boxes she was carrying. The top one started to fall. Melissa dove for it and caught it handily.

"Mrs. Wyman's timing is perfect, as usual," she said with a sigh. "I'll go and find out what she wants." As she passed Ms Rachlis, she said, "That's one thing you won't miss, right, Nat? All that thumping."

Ms Rachlis didn't answer. She went into the kitchen to tape and label the two boxes. Melissa returned a few moments later.

"I told Mrs. Wyman you were leaving," she said to Ms Rachlis. "She wants to see you so that she can say goodbye. Come on. I'll go with you so that she doesn't talk your ear off."

"I'll vacuum while you're gone," I said.

"The vacuum cleaner is in the bedroom closet," Melissa said.

The two of them disappeared again. As I got out the vacuum cleaner and started to set it up, I heard something — a phone — ringing in the distance. It sounded as if it was coming from across the hall. It must be Melissa's phone. I wondered if I should answer it for her, but decided against it. If it was important, whoever it was would either call back or leave a message.

I hooked up the vacuum cleaner and started in the bedroom. Then I moved into the kitchen, but the cord wouldn't reach any farther, so I went into the bedroom to unplug it, carried the cord into the living room, and looked for another outlet. Soon dirt and dust and, yes, tobacco, were being sucked into the vacuum-cleaner bag. The carpet started to change from a greyish colour to a cream colour right before my eyes. Too bad Ms Rachlis didn't use her vacuum cleaner more often.

I moved back and forth across the room — until suddenly my foot caught on the vacuum-cleaner cord and I lost my balance. I staggered backward into a pile of boxes, pushing the top one over. It hadn't been sealed. Some of the contents spilled out — a fabric-covered box; two decorative tins, the kind I use to store pens and pencils, hair clips, and little mementos that would otherwise get lost; and several envelopes of photographs. Photographs slid out, cascading across the floor. I picked up the box and the two tins and then started to gather the photos.

"It's okay, I'll get those," Ms Rachlis said, startling me. I hadn't heard her return. She came into the living room. Behind her, in the kitchen, Melissa was looking at the answering machine. She said, "You've got a message, Nat."

"It's from yesterday," Ms Rachlis said listlessly. "It's probably a telemarketer. It always is."

"Your phone rang, too, Melissa," I said. "While you were downstairs."

Ms Rachlis bent down and began picking up the photos that were strewn across the floor.

"It might not be a telemarketer this time, Nat. It might be something important," Melissa said. "Maybe the police. We should check." Her voice was perky in contrast to Ms Rachlis's. She was trying so hard to cheer her up. "How does this work?" she said. "Oh. Okay. Rewind." There was a pause. "Play," she said triumphantly.

I heard a *tchonk*, the sound of the tape on the answering machine stopping after being rewound, then a click, followed by a man's voice: "I want to talk to her myself. You talking to her is not doing any good. I am tired of waiting . . . "

Ms Rachlis straightened up abruptly, leaving a lot of photographs on the floor. She turned slowly toward the answering machine in the kitchen.

"That's an old message," she said. "I meant to erase it." She walked swiftly into the kitchen.

I looked down at the photos that Ms Rachlis hadn't collected.

A few of them caught my eye and I bent to pick them up.

I glanced into the kitchen. Melissa was staring at the answering machine, her mouth open. She looked dazed. "That's Mikhail's voice," she said.

I heard another *tchonk* and the voice stopped. Ms Rachlis was standing at the machine now, her finger on the Stop button.

"I don't understand," Melissa said. "He called you? Mikhail called you and you didn't tell me? What was he talking about? What did you tell him, Nat?"

I looked at the pictures I was holding — Ms Rachlis, a little younger than she was now, beaming, her arm around a man — Mikhail Mornov — whose arm was around her. Ms Rachlis kissing Mikhail Mornov on the cheek, Ms Rachlis holding Mikhail Mornov's hand. Ms Rachlis obviously in love. If she thought he was trouble and if she had warned Melissa about him, why did she have these pictures? Then I saw more pictures — or, rather, half pictures: the same man, Mikhail Mornov, smiling fondly at someone, but that person had been cut out of the pictures. In some, Mikhail Mornov's hand had been sliced off, too. In others, a disembodied woman's hand lingered on his shoulder. In one photo, a ring was clearly visible on that hand. I would have recognized it anywhere. It was the ring Ted had passed down to Melissa.

"Melissa?" I said, holding out the pictures. But she was focused one hundred percent on Ms Rachlis.

"I want to hear what he said, Nat," she said. Her voice was shrill. I heard the muffled sound of a phone ringing across the hall, but Melissa didn't seem to notice. She pushed Ms Rachlis aside and hit the answering machine's Play button to hear the rest of the message. The man's voice continued: "You said you would help me, but I'm tired of waiting and now she's going to marry that man. I'm going to talk to her myself."

My cell phone rang, making me jump.

I fumbled for it in my pocket and answered it just as Ms Rachlis grabbed the answering machine and yanked it away from Melissa. Its electrical cord came out of the wall socket.

"Robyn?" the voice on the phone said. "It's Ted."

"Ted, I — "

Melissa turned to look at me.

"I've been trying to reach Melissa, but she doesn't answer," Ted said. "Do you think she might be at school? I just got a call from the police. They're having second thoughts about what happened. They say the only call to my condo the night Mornov was shot came from Natalie Rachlis's apartment. Now they're wondering what really happened. I think they think that Melissa — "

Ms Rachlis ripped the phone out of my hand and jammed her thumb down on the Off button. My first instinct was to try to grab the phone back from her. But I rejected that course of action almost immediately, mostly because of the knife. It was long and heavy and sharp. It was also much too close to my throat. I stared at it while Ms Rachlis shoved my phone into her pocket. But out of the corner of my eye I saw Melissa edging toward the apartment door.

"Take one more step and you'll be saying goodbye to your future stepsister forever," Ms Rachlis said. She grabbed me and held me in front of her. I felt the point of the knife pierce the skin of my neck. "Come here, Melissa," she said.

Melissa hesitated.

"I'm not kidding," Ms Rachlis said, her voice as sharp and cold as the blade of the knife.

Melissa walked slowly toward us.

My knees started to buckle. As I sagged, I felt a pinpoint of searing pain in my neck. Melissa's face went pale. She was staring at the knife and at me. I felt something trickle down my neck and felt weak all over again. Blood. It had to be blood.

"Nat, please — " Melissa said.

"Bring me that tape," Ms Rachlis said to her.

Melissa looked wildly around the kitchen.

"Just the tape, Melissa," Ms Rachlis said. She pressed the knife against my neck again.

Melissa picked up the roll of duct tape that was sitting on the kitchen table.

"That's it," Ms Rachlis said. "Now bring it here."

Melissa obeyed.

"Lie down," Ms Rachlis commanded. Melissa hesitated. Again I felt the prick of the knife. Melissa dropped to her knees. "Face down," Ms Rachlis said.

"Nat, please — "

"Do it, Melissa," Ms Rachlis said. "You've already ruined everything. I'm not going to let you destroy the rest of my life."

Melissa lay down on the carpet that I had just vacuumed.

Ms Rachlis released her grip on me. She thrust the tape into my hand.

"Fasten her hands behind her back with this," she said. "And make it tight."

"Nat, I don't understand," Melissa said. "Why did Mikhail call you? And what did he mean when he said that you talking to me wasn't doing any good?"

"Hurry up," Ms Rachlis said to me.

My hands were shaking as I wrapped layer after layer of sturdy tape around Melissa's wrists. What had Ted been saying when Ms Rachlis yanked my phone from my hands? The only call to his place that night had come from here, from Ms Rachlis's apartment.

"That was Ted on the phone," I said. "When Mikhail called you at Ted's place, he was calling from here."

"Mikhail was here?" Melissa said.

"Now her mouth," Ms Rachlis said. "Tape her mouth."

My mind raced as I did what I was told. I thought about the photographs I had just seen — photos of Mikhail and Ms Rachlis together, as well as what had obviously been photographs of Mikhail and Melissa together, except that someone had sliced them in half, cutting Melissa away from Mikhail. I thought about the little sketches of flowers that I had found in the scrap-paper bin in the art room — sketches that were similar, I now realized, to the drawing on the label of the flower box from the non-existent Garden of Eden. I though about seeing Mikhail in front of the school — twice, the second time raising his hand to wave to someone after Melissa had already driven away with Ted. I'd have bet anything that he'd been waiting for Ms Rachlis — the only other person he knew at my school. I thought about the tactics Mikhail had supposedly used to scare Melissa. They were almost identical to the tactics James Duguid had used to terrorize Melissa's mother. But Melissa had said that she hadn't told Mikhail what her mother had been through. She'd told very few people. But she had told Ms Rachlis, which meant that Ms Rachlis knew exactly what to do to not only scare Melissa and make her believe that Mikhail was stalking her, but also to stir up horrific memories from her childhood.

I looked at Melissa, her wrists, ankles, and mouth firmly bound with duct tape, and thought about the night she'd shot Mikhail. Ms Rachlis told the police that he had turned up at her apartment after she got back from Ted's. She said he'd cornered her in the *kitchen*. But all those bits of tobacco proved that he had been sitting on a chair in the living room. And I knew now that he had been here while Melissa, Ms Rachlis, and I were at Ted's place. He had called Melissa from here.

Bit by bit, it was making sense.

I turned to Ms Rachlis. "Ted's phone number is unlisted," I said, trying to keep my voice steady. "But you knew it. Melissa gave it to you. You called Mikhail before we went over to Ted's and you gave him the phone number, didn't you? You told him he could reach Melissa there. You probably even suggested that he call her. You knew it would scare her."

But it wasn't just the phone call that had done it. There was also the note. The security guard hadn't let anyone into the building. The security cameras hadn't caught anyone, either. I had assumed that this proved how clever — and how dangerous — Mikhail Mornov was. Now I saw that I had been wrong.

"*You* slipped that note under the mat," I said. My heart was hammering in my chest. "That's why the security cameras didn't pick up anyone sneaking into the building. Mikhail was never in the building. But you were. You're the one who found the note because you're the one who slipped it under the mat after Melissa and I had already gone inside." I glanced at Melissa. Her eyes were wide with realization. "*And* you sent those flowers," I said. Ms Rachlis's face was a mask of fury and hatred. What was she going to do?

213

What could *I* do to try to stop her? "You sent those flowers to Melissa to scare her. You also trashed her car. Mikhail had an alibi, but I bet if the police checked it out, they'd find that you didn't."

Ms Rachlis lunged at me and grabbed my hair. She yanked it hard. I let out a howl, for all the good it would do me. The only person around was deaf old Mrs. Wyman downstairs. Ms Rachlis held fast to me while she tested how well I had secured Melissa's hands. Then she ordered me to lie down. She knelt on top of me, one of her knees jammed into the small of my back. I grunted with pain. She grabbed my right arm and twisted it hard behind my back. She had to set the knife down to take hold of my left arm and force it behind me, too. She adjusted her knee so that now it was pressed down on my crossed arms. The pain was so sharp that tears welled up in my eyes. I felt her weight shift a little as she reached for the tape. If I could get her off me . . . I tried to roll to one side, but she put her full weight on me and grabbed the knife.

"Try that again and I'll cut you, I swear I will," she said. I felt the tip of the knife between my shoulder blades, and I froze. Again I felt her weight shift a little. Then I heard the *kkkttt* of the tape. She began to bind my wrists.

"I saw those pictures. You knew Mikhail Mornov before Melissa started going out with him," I said. "Did you go out with him, too? Did he dump you? Is that it? Or did you want to go out with him and he wasn't interested in you? I know how that feels." If I

214

could establish a connection with her — any connection — maybe it would help. "I know how it hurts."

"I wish you'd killed him," Ms Rachlis said bitterly, her eyes fixed on Melissa. "I hope he dies. It would serve him right. You, too. You'd have to live with that for the rest of your life."

Melissa was staring at her as if she were seeing her for the first time. My mind exploded with memories of what happened that night.

"You tricked Melissa," I said. "When she showed up here that night, you tricked her. Mikhail didn't threaten you, either. He was trying to get downstairs to see Melissa. He didn't want to hurt her. And you tried to stop him. That's why he had the knife. You — "

"She ruined everything," Ms Rachlis said. "It's all her fault. He was mine. He was interested in me right up until he met *her*. I introduced them. I went to that party to see him. I brought Melissa along because I felt sorry for her. She never went anywhere. She was always so afraid. I introduced them, and the next thing I knew, I ran into them together and Mikhail was telling me what a good friend I was to have fixed him up with a girl like Melissa. That's what he kept calling me. *Friend*. As if I was never special to him." She pulled off more tape to bind me even more securely.

What was she going to do? Was she planning to kill us? I thought about Ted — was he trying to contact me again? Was he worried because he couldn't? Was he worried enough to have called the police? Maybe if I could keep her talking . . .

"You knew all about Melissa's mother and you used that to scare her," I said. The weight lifted from my back. Ms Rachlis stood up. "You told her lies about Mikhail. You made him out to be a stalker. You scared Melissa right out of town, didn't you?"

I thought about the phone message that Melissa had just played back.

"But he really loved her. He wanted to find her and you offered to help." That had to be it. It was the only way his phone message made sense.

Ms Rachlis reached for the tape and ripped off a piece. She pressed it over my mouth and slowly stood up.

"Get up," she said. She grabbed a hank of my hair and jerked me onto my feet. "You, too, Melissa. Get up."

Melissa stumbled to her feet. Ms Rachlis gripped me from behind and held the knife to my throat again.

"We're going to go down the back stairs and into the basement," Ms Rachlis said. "You're going to lead the way, Melissa. If you try anything, if you do anything other than what I tell you to do, Robyn is going to get hurt. Badly. You understand?"

Melissa nodded.

Ms Rachlis opened the apartment door and we went out into the hall. Melissa led the way down the stairs. Ms Rachlis held tightly to me. The whole way she pressed the knife against my throat. On the last flight of stairs, the one that led down into a gloomy, unfinished basement, I stumbled and felt the knife slice through my skin. My whole body turned to ice. I felt blood run down my neck. How badly had she cut me? Would I bleed to death? But Ms Rachlis kept forcing me downward until finally we were in the basement. She reached up and pulled a chain that switched on a light. The place was piled with trunks and boxes. A massive oil-burning furnace occupied one whole corner. There was a door beside it. Ms Rachlis moved us toward it, opened it, and peered inside. The small, dark room smelled musty.

"That'll do," she said. "Get in there."

She shoved Melissa in and dragged me by the hair.

"Lie down," she said. When Melissa hesitated, Ms Rachlis pressed the knife against my throat again. I winced. Melissa knelt down. Ms Rachlis planted one foot on Melissa's back and forced her face down onto the filthy concrete. "You should be grateful to Robyn and that boyfriend of hers," she said to Melissa. "If they hadn't shown up when they did, Mikhail would be dead, and I would have denied that he was threatening me. I would have told the police that you shot him in cold blood, that you murdered him. It would have been your word against mine — and with your past, who do you think they would have believed?" She twisted my hair. "Now you," she said. "Down."

I sank down beside Melissa. Ms Rachlis bound our ankles with duct tape. Then she closed the door to the room. We heard noises outside, heavy boxes or trunks being dragged and stacked across the front of the door.

Then silence.

* * *

We lay there for a few minutes, neither of us moving, neither of us even able to see in the darkness. Then I felt Melissa squirm up against me. She was breathing hard. My eyes adjusted. I could make her out, but just barely. She was sitting up now and nodding her head. At first I couldn't figure out what she was doing. Then I understood: she wanted me to sit up, too. I wriggled my way to a sitting position. Melissa kept moving her head to one side, as if she were trying to tell me something. It was only when she started to work her way around so that her back was to me that I got the idea. I did the same. We pressed our bound hands up against each other. I felt her picking at the tape around my wrists. Picking and picking, but not getting anywhere. She couldn't find the end of it, and without that, there was no way that she would be able to get it off. I pushed against her, hard. She went rigid. Then I started picking at her tape. Ms Rachlis had bound me, but I had bound Melissa and I had sealed the tape at the back. I felt for the edge with my fingernail and found it. I began to pick at it as best as I could with sore and twisted hands. It was like trying to carry a bucket of water up a mountain one drop at a time. I picked and picked. Finally I had an end loose. We both had to manoeuvre so that I could start to unravel it millimetre by aching millimetre until finally her hands pulled free. A moment later she said, "Robyn, are you okay?"

I nodded.

I felt a hand pick at the corner of the tape across my mouth.

"This might hurt," she said. She pulled the tape from my mouth. Then she worked the tape off my wrists. We freed our ankles.

But we couldn't budge the door.

We shouted.

Nothing.

We threw our shoulders against the door — and were rewarded with bruised shoulders.

"Do you think Ms Rachlis is still up there?" I said at last.

"I don't know."

"Do you think she's going to come back down here?"

"I don't know," she said. "I don't know."

* * *

Ms Rachlis didn't come back. After a while, we started to hammer on the door. We tried everything we could to open it. We kicked it. We pried at it. We kicked it some more. We yelled. We screamed until we were hoarse. We sank down to the floor.

"It's a sturdy old house," Melissa said, "and it's so far away from the road and the neighbours' yards. I don't think anyone will hear us — unless one of them happens to come right up to the house, and that hardly ever happens. For sure Mrs. Wyman won't hear us."

My heart pounded in my chest. I felt like crying, but forced myself to hold my tears in.

"How long do you think we've been down here?" I said finally.

"I don't know. Over an hour, I think." She fumbled

with her watch — I saw it glow fleetingly. "Three hours. Maybe a little more," she said, sounding surprised.

"Does Mrs. Wyman have a newspaper delivered to her house?" Worst case, we could wait until morning and try to attract the attention of the newspaper delivery person.

"No," Melissa said. "And neither do Nat or I. And anyway, tomorrow is Sunday."

My throat got tight. I couldn't breathe. I knew what it was — panic — but knowing it didn't make me feel any better. I got up and kicked at the door again and again and again, until my foot hurt and my knee was throbbing from the brutal impact of my foot hammering, hammering, hammering into the door.

"Robyn."

I couldn't stop kicking and kicking.

"Robyn." Melissa grabbed my arm.

I started to cry. I couldn't help it.

Melissa hugged me.

"I'm sorry," she said. "I'm sorry I got you caught up in all of this."

"It's not your fault," I said. I forced myself to draw in a deep breath to calm myself. Then another. "It's not your fault."

Melissa was silent for a few moments. Then, "I trusted her," she said. "I trusted the wrong person." She let out a long and shuddering sigh.

"Someone will come looking for us," she said. She tried to sound upbeat, but it seemed forced to me. "Ted called, didn't he? And he was cut off. He'll be worried about you. So will your mother. They'll look for you."

"They'll look for us," I said.

Chapter 18

"What time is it?" I said.

Melissa checked her watch again. "It's after midnight."

We had been sitting on the floor in the tiny room for hours. My stomach was rumbling, but that didn't bother me as much as my dry mouth. I hadn't had anything to drink since morning, before I'd gone shopping. I knew that humans could last for days, even weeks, without food. But water is a different story. Water is a necessity.

I got up and started feeling my way around the small room. It was some kind of storeroom — boxes were stacked against one wall. But all they contained were books. Useless. Everything in the small room was utterly useless.

"Someone will find us," Melissa said. But it sounded more like a hope than a promise.

It was cold in the dark, windowless room. We huddled together, but that didn't help my feet, which were turning to ice. Melissa shivered beside me.

"The house is drafty and the basement is cold," she said, "but the furnace is on. We may be uncomfortable, but we won't freeze."

"Does Mrs. Wyman ever come down here?" I asked.

"I don't know," Melissa said.

She didn't come down that night.

No one did.

Every so often we got up and stomped our feet to stay warm. We whooped and shouted, hoping that someone would hear us.

No one did.

Eventually I fell asleep.

* * *

I heard a skittering sound. My eyes shot open. The thought that ripped through my brain: Rats.

I nudged Melissa.

She jolted awake.

The sound had stopped.

"It's nothing," I said. "What time is it?"

She peered at her watch.

"Nearly noon."

Then I heard it again. What I thought was the sound of ratty little feet on concrete was now getting fainter and fainter. My first thought was relief. My next thought: Help! Help! We're here! I started to pound on the door.

For a moment I heard nothing. Then I heard a welcome sound, muffled and barely audible.

"Robbie? Robbie, are you there?"

"Dad! Melissa's here with me."

We waited, listening to my father shout for someone and then listening to grunts and bangs as whoever was out there with him worked with him to clear the door.

Finally, the door swung open and my father stepped into the room. I threw myself into his arms. Ted came in behind him, his eyes nervous and afraid until they lit on Melissa and he saw that she was fine. He embraced her.

"I was worried," Ted said. "We couldn't figure out where you were. You just disappeared."

"Your mother was frantic," my father said. "There was a message waiting on my phone when I got in from the airport. She and Ted looked everywhere."

"Everywhere except the basement," Ted said sheepishly. "That was Ben's idea."

"Ben?" I said.

My father nodded over his shoulder. "Your mother called him to see if he'd heard from you. He drove around all night looking for you."

I spotted Ben's pale face behind my father. He smiled at me.

* * *

Things were chaotic after that. My father called my mother and the police — in that order — and then ushered us all back upstairs to Melissa's apartment to wait for them. Melissa asked if there was any news about Mikhail.

"The police told me yesterday, before I called Robyn, that he had regained consciousness," Ted said. "They've listed his condition as serious, but they're optimistic that he's going to make a good recovery."

"Thank goodness," Melissa said. There were tears in her eyes.

My father asked me over and over if I was okay. Only when he seemed satisfied that the nicks on my neck weren't serious and Ted had made us some tea so that we could warm up did my father get around to explaining how they had found us.

"It was Ben's idea to come back to the house," he said. "He figured that if Melissa was missing too, then the two of you were probably together. We searched the apartment and found your purse in one of the closets, which told us that you had been here. So we went up and down the street, talking to all the neighbours again to see if anyone had seen either of you. We found a couple of people we hadn't spoken to last night. One of them thought she saw you walk up the street yesterday afternoon. But no one saw you or Melissa leave the house. Then we spoke to a man who had been out all night. He said that as he was leaving his house last night, he saw a taxi come out of Mrs. Wyman's driveway."

"Nat," Melissa said.

"Most likely," my father said. "Anyway, after we had that piece of information, Ben insisted that we search the one place we hadn't checked — the basement."

I look at him, surprised. "What made you think of that?"

He shrugged. "I remembered you telling me that the woman who lives here is practically deaf. And this house is quite a distance from the road and from the neighbouring houses. I thought it was worth a try."

My father smiled. "He'd make a terrific police officer." I got up and went to sit beside Ben. He put his arm around me, and I nestled against him. My father waited a few moments before he said, "What exactly happened, Robbie?"

* * *

I had just finished telling the whole story to Charlie Hart when someone knocked on the door of the small room where we were sitting. Charlie Hart reached out and switched off the video recorder.

"Excuse me for a minute, Robyn," he said. He got up and left the room. He was back a minute later. "They arrested Natalie Rachlis in Montreal. She was about to board a plane."

What a relief.

"I think we're finished for now, Robyn," he said. "I'll let you know if I need to ask you any more questions."

* * *

Ben was waiting with my parents. He promised them that he'd have me safely back in time for a late supper. He took me downtown to a fancy restaurant where we got a seat in the window.

"I thought you'd appreciate a view after being shut up in that basement all night," he said. He flagged a waiter and ordered hot chocolate for both of us and a plate of teacakes. After the waiter left, I pulled out the bag that my father had retrieved from Ms Denholm's closet.

"I got you a little something for Valentine's Day," I said, handing him the chocolates. "And this," I handed him the other box, "is for your sister."

"Thank you," he said. "And I have something for you. I've been carrying it around ever since I picked it up a couple of weeks ago. I wanted to give it to you right away, but . . . " He reached into his pocket and brought out a small box tied with a white ribbon. He handed it to me.

My fingers trembled as I opened it.

"Oh, Ben," I said, staring into the box. Nestled in blue velvet was a gold ring, set with three pearls. "It's so beautiful. Thank you."

Ben took the ring from the box and slipped it onto my finger.

"It fits perfectly," I said.

"Happy Valentine's Day," he said. He leaned over the table and kissed me lightly on the lips.

I reached behind me and undid the clasp on the chain that Nick had given me. I removed it and the intertwined hearts from my neck and dropped them onto the table.

"Happy Valentine's Day to you, too, Ben," I said.

We held hands until our hot chocolate arrived.

Chapter 19

I stayed home from school the next day and spent almost all of it sleeping. That night, for the first time since my parents had divorced, the two of them sat at the same table and shared a meal. Not alone, of course. Ted was there. So were Melissa and I. And Ben. We were all gathered in one of the private dining rooms at La Folie. By then my father had worked his contacts and had got all the details, and Ted had taken Melissa to the hospital to see Mikhail. "I can't believe that Nat did all those terrible things. I really trusted her," Melissa said. "I knew that she and Mikhail had gone out briefly. He told me. But I never knew that she was in love with him. He told me it was just casual."

"She resented the way he fell so fast for you," my father said. Melissa blushed. "He even introduced you to his parents, didn't he?" She nodded. "He never introduced Natalie. She resented that, too. She also resented the fact that he always referred to her as an old friend. And, of course, she resented you for coming between her and Mikhail."

"But I didn't know," Melissa said. "No one told me."

"She played on your experience with your mother to try to drive you and Mikhail apart," Ted said.

Melissa nodded. "The whole time she was pretending to be supportive of both me and Mikhail — the whole time — she was doing everything she could to make sure we stayed apart. And it worked. She scared me so badly that I left town."

"But Mikhail refused to give up," Ted said gently. "He really seems to love you."

Melissa's eyes glistened with tears. "He told me that today. He said he was so confused. He couldn't understand why I treated him the way I did. Then when Nat told him about my mother . . . " Her voice trailed off. It took her a few moments to compose herself. "Some guys would have been scared off, but not Mikhail. He said it made everything come clear to him. He wanted to talk to me, to try to reassure me he wasn't like James."

"When he finally located you, he wanted to come and see you himself," my father said. "But Natalie convinced him that was a bad idea. She said you would run away again. She offered to help him."

"He trusted her, too," Melissa said bitterly.

My father nodded. "After Mikhail told the police what really happened, Nat came clean. According to Charlie, she told Mikhail that she'd come here ahead of him and would talk to you and see how you were doing. That's why she was suddenly interested in a job here. She told Charlie she arranged a job for herself so that she could be close to you."

"What do you mean?" Melissa said.

"Natalie Rachlis is responsible for the regular art teacher's 'accident.' She did everything she could to put herself in close contact with you."

Melissa's face turned white. "I recommended her to the principal."

"She's a real manipulator," my father said. "But she must have known that Mikhail wouldn't wait forever and that he'd eventually turn up here."

"That's why she started scaring me again," Melissa said. She shook her head. "She wanted me to run and hide just like my mother did."

Ted reached across the table and laid one of his hands on hers.

"She used Ted, too," my father said. "She told Mikhail that you'd met someone else. She said that you were going to marry Ted. It nearly worked. Mikhail said he was happy for you. But he wanted to talk to you one last time. And when Ted reacted the way he did, he wanted to set things straight. He didn't want you to be afraid of him."

"Meanwhile, Natalie was terrorizing me and pretending it was Mikhail," Melissa said.

"She almost got away with it," I said.

Melissa nodded. "I almost ran. I was so scared of everyone." She looked at my father. "The first time I saw you looking at my car in the parking lot at school, I thought you were working for Mikhail." My father shrugged apologetically. "But then I thought about my mother. She ran. She hid. And for the rest of her life she was afraid to go out, afraid to be herself, afraid of everyone. I didn't want to live that way."

"After you decided to confront Mikhail, you called Natalie from your car and told her you were returning to your apartment, didn't you?"

Melissa nodded. "She didn't pick up, so I left a message. I told her that I wasn't going to let Mikhail scare me anymore. That I was through running."

"According to what Mikhail told the police, Mrs. Wyman banged on the ceiling and Natalie went down to see what she wanted. She was downstairs when you called. When Natalie's answering machine picked up the message, Mikhail heard what you were saying. He wanted to pick up the phone himself and tell you that you had nothing to be afraid of, but he thought maybe that would scare you. He decided to wait and talk to you in person. I'm not sure how much he figured out, but it was enough to make him decide to confront Natalie when she came back upstairs. They got into a fight."

"We heard them when we got back to the house," I said.

"Mikhail saw you drive up," my father said. "He wanted to go down and talk to Melissa, but Natalie tried to stop him. With a knife."

I shuddered when he said that. I remembered the feel of that knife against my neck.

"Natalie turned the tables on him. She started screaming that he was trying to kill her."

"And when I saw him holding that knife . . . " Melissa said.

"He'd wrestled it away from Natalie. He was afraid she might try to hurt you."

"And I rewarded him by shooting him," Melissa said in a whisper.

"You thought you were saving a friend's life," Ted said.

Melissa looked at Ben. "If you hadn't been there — "

"His doctor says he's doing well," Ted said, reaching for her hand.

"But if Ben hadn't done what he did . . . " Melissa whispered.

My father looked directly at her. "Natalie didn't know you had the gun, did she?"

Melissa shook her head. "She tried to make me leave it at Ted's. And she never thought I'd go back to the apartment."

"But you took the gun with you."

"Yes."

"Natalie told the police she knew she was never going to win him back," my father said. "Once she knew you were on your way back to the apartment, her plan was to accuse him of trying to kill her. She knew you'd back her up. It would have been the two of you against him. He'd go to prison. She wouldn't have had him, but neither would you. When you shot him, she was stunned. At first, she said, she couldn't believe it."

"He never meant me any harm," Melissa murmured.

Ted squeezed her hand.

"You didn't know that."

"I should have trusted him. I shouldn't have been afraid," Melissa said, tears glistening in her eyes. "I'm never going to run away again. I saw what it did to Mom. That's not going to happen to me. I'm going to trust people. I'm going to trust Mikhail."

"You may need help, Melissa," my mother said gently. "It's hard trying to break the habits of a life-time."

Melissa nodded. But she looked determined.

* * *

After the meal was over, Ted flagged down a taxi for Melissa. I walked Ben to the door and said good night to him. He promised to call me the next day.

After he'd driven away, my mother pulled me aside.

"Do you mind staying with your father tonight?" she said.

"How come?"

"Ted says he wants to talk to me about something. And after everything that's happened — "

"No problem, Mom," I said.

* * *

The next morning when I got up, I found my father sitting on the sofa, staring out the window and sipping coffee. He glanced at me, but he didn't say anything.

"Are you okay, Dad?" I said.

He nodded, but the gesture was stiff. Something was wrong.

"You sure you're okay, Dad?"

"Your mother called while you were in the shower."

The phone rang.

"Maybe that's her now," I said. I headed for the phone.

"She called *me*," my father said. "She said she wanted to tell me before I heard it from someone else."

"Heard what?"

The phone rang again.

"She's getting married," my father said. He swallowed a mouthful of coffee. He looked miserable. I felt sorry for him.

The phone rang yet again. He glanced at it.

"Get that for me, will you, Robbie?" he said. "If it's Vern, I'll take it. Otherwise . . . "

I picked up the phone on the next ring. "Hello?"

"I've been calling you and calling you," Morgan said. She sounded breathless. "You don't answer your cell. I finally called your mom."

"I lost my phone," I said. I had no idea what Ms Rachlis had done with it. The police hadn't found it. "I — "

Morgan cut me off. "Guess who Billy swears he saw Sunday afternoon after we got back into town?" She answered before I could say a word. "Nick. He swears he saw Nick."

My heart started to pound.

"Is he sure?"

"He says he is. After we got off the bus on Sunday,

I went home and Billy went to the DARC office to drop off some things. He was walking down the street and he says he saw you and Ben in the window of a restaurant. He says he waved at you, but you were too busy talking to Ben and you didn't see him. He says he caught a reflection in the window and turned and there was Nick, standing right across the street."

I felt cold all over. "What was he doing?"

"The same thing Billy was doing. He was staring at you. Billy says he waved to him, but that Nick just turned and walked away."

Oh.

Other great books
by Norah McClintock

Robyn Hunter Mysteries
Last Chance
You Can Run
Nothing to Lose
Out of the Cold

Chloe and Levesque Mysteries
The Third Degree
Over the Edge
Double Cross
Scared to Death
Break and Enter
No Escape
Not a Trace

Mike and Riel Mysteries
Hit and Run
Truth and Lies
Dead and Gone
Seeing and Believing
Dead Silence

Also available
Body, Crime, Suspect
The Body in the Basement
Password: Murder
Mistaken Identity